THE
INTERREX

Also by CATHERINE FISHER

THE SNOW-WALKER SEQUENCE
The Snow-Walker's Son
The Empty Hand
The Soul Thieves

The Conjuror's Game
Fintan's Tower
The Candle Man
Belin's Hill

THE BOOK OF THE CROW
The Relic Master
Flain's Coronet
The Margrave

CATHERINE FISHER

THE INTERREX

RED FOX

To Maggie and Roger

A Red Fox Book

Published by Random House Children's Books
20 Vauxhall Bridge Road, London SW1V 2SA

A division of The Random House Group Ltd
London Melbourne Sydney Auckland
Johannesburg and agencies throughout the world

1 3 5 7 9 10 8 6 4 2

First published in Great Britain by The Bodley Head Children's Books 1999

This Red Fox edition 2001

Printed and bound in Great Britain
by Bookmarque Ltd, Croydon, Surrey.

Papers used by The Random House Group Ltd are natural, recyclable products made from wood grown in sustainable forests. The manufacturing processes conform to the environmental regulations of the country of origin.

THE RANDOM HOUSE GROUP Limited Reg. No. 954009
www.randomhouse.co.uk

ISBN 0 09 926394 7

Contents

Flainsdeath   5

Games of Chance   37

The Tower of Song   65

Artelan's Well   109

Standing in Line   153

The Falls of Keilder   187

The strain on his arms was agony. Clutching the rope, he hauled himself up, hand over hand, gripping with aching knees and ankles.

'Hurry up!' The Sekoi leaned precariously from the tower ledge above, its seven fingers stretching for him. Behind it the Maker-wall glimmered in the light of the moons.

Raffi gave one last desperate pull, flung his hand up and grabbed. A hard grip clenched on his; he was dragged on to the ledge and clung there, gasping and soaked with sweat.

'Not bad,' the creature purred in his ear. 'Now look down.'

Below them, the night was black. Somewhere at the tower's smooth base Galen was waiting, a shadow with a hooked face of moonlight, staring up. Even from here Raffi could feel his tension.

'Now what?' he hissed.

'The window.' Delicately, the Sekoi put its long hand out and wriggled it through the smashed, patched pane. A latch clicked. The casement creaked softly open.

The creature's fur tickled Raffi as it whispered, 'In you go.'

Raffi nodded. Silently he swung his feet in and slithered over the sill, standing in the still room.

1

In the moonlight he sent a sense-line out, feeling at once the tangled dreams of the man in the bed, the sleeping bodyguards outside the door, and then, as he groped for it, the bright mind-echo of the relic, the familiar blue box.

It was somewhere near the bed.

He pointed; the Sekoi nodded, its yellow eyes catching the light. Raffi began to cross the room. He knew there was no one else here, but if Alberic woke up and yelled there soon would be. The tiny man seemed lost in the vast bed, its hangings purple and crimson damask, heavy and expensive. Probably stolen. Beside the bed was a table, a dim shadow of smooth wood, and he could just see the gleam of a drawer-handle. The relic box was in there.

Galen's box.

Inch by inch, Raffi's hand moved towards the drawer.

Alberic snuffled, turned over. His face was close to Raffi now; a sly face, even in sleep. Soundlessly, Raffi opened the drawer, pushed his fingers in and touched the box. Power jerked through him; his fingers clenched on it and he almost hissed with the shock. Then it was out, and shoved deep inside his jerkin.

Glancing back, he saw the Sekoi's black shape breathless against the window; behind it the stars were bright. He backed, carefully.

But Alberic was restless, turning and tossing in his rich covers; with each step back Raffi felt the dwarf's sharp mind bubbling up out of the dark, a growing unease. As he turned and grabbed the window he felt the moment of waking like a pain.

Alberic sat bolt upright. He stared across the dark room; in that instant he saw them both, and a strangled scream of fury broke out of him. In

2

seconds Raffi was out, slithering down the rope after the Sekoi, so fast that the heat seared the gloves on his hands, and as he hit the bottom and crumpled to his knees he heard the dogs erupt into barking and the screeching of Alberic's wrath.

Galen's hand grabbed him. 'Have you got it?'

'Yes!'

The dwarf's head jutted from the high window. 'Galen Harn!' he screamed, his voice raw. 'And you, Sekoi! I'll kill you both for this!'

He seemed to be demented with rage; someone had to haul him back inside. 'I'll kill you!' he shrieked.

But the night was dark. They were already long gone.

Flainsdeath

1

*As the Makers shaped the world, Kest
began to brood in his secret place,
remembering the scorn of Flain and
Tamar's jokes. And in a cave under the
ice he began his experiments, making tiny
beasts from parts of others, giving them
forbidden life. And these things he kept
hidden from Flain's wrath.*

Book of the Seven Moons

'Are you sure you've got everything?' Rocallion
asked anxiously.

Raffi finished arranging the black and green
beads and looked round. 'Maybe a few more
candles.'

'I'll get them sent up. Will the keeper be ready?'

They both glanced across the dim room. Galen
was sitting by the fire, in an upright chair. He
seemed to be day-dreaming, staring deep into the
flames, but when Raffi reached out for the keeper's
soul, he couldn't find it; it was walking far away in
some place he hadn't yet learned to reach. 'He'll
be ready in his own time.'

Rocallion nodded, pulling berries nervously off
the holly. He was a young man to be franklin of
so big a manor, Raffi thought, but he seemed to
run it well. The fields they'd travelled through yesterday had been well-ploughed, the cottages in
good repair. And now Rocallion was worried; it
made Raffi worry too.

'No more news of the Watch?' Raffi asked.

7

Rocallion perched on the edge of the bench. He nearly put the holly berry in his mouth, then tossed it absently into the fire. 'Only the rumour of that patrol out at Tarnos. That was two days ago. Before the leaf-fall.' He gazed out at the darkening sky. 'It should keep them indoors. But on Flainsnight, you never know.'

Raffi nodded, crossing to the window and leaning his hands on the sill. He knew that whatever the weather the Watch would be prowling tonight. In the damp chill of the autumn twilight the countryside beyond was misty, the far hills faint blurs. In the cloud-ragged sky the moons were bright, all seven of them, with Pyra a fiery-red point in the east. There were no other lights, anywhere.

'Raffi!'

He turned, instantly.

Galen was standing, tall and dark, his hawk-face sharp in the firelight. Power was moving around him; Raffi could see it, the blue tingles and sparks. It made him shiver.

'I'm ready,' the keeper said softly. 'Let them in.'

The room was dark, as it should be, with no light but the fire. As the door opened Raffi saw the shapes of Rocallion's tenants slip into the room, twelve or so men, the ones he could trust, with their wives and a few children. In the dimness they were nervous shadows, the creak of a bench, a whisper.

The air of the room was sharp with sorcery and fear. All of them knew that if the Watch caught them they'd pay heavily. Money, cattle, even their children might be taken away. Rocallion would lose most. But they wouldn't die, Raffi thought bitterly. Not like he and Galen would die. Slowly.

He shivered. But Galen had begun.

'Friends. This is the night of Flainsdeath. Tonight we do what the faithful have done for centuries, since the Makers themselves were here.' He frowned. 'In these days of evil we have to meet in secret; I salute the courage of each of you in coming. Tonight the Watch will ride out. But if you have kept the secret, we may be safe.'

His black eyes watched their tense faces. So did Raffi.

They were scared. That was natural. Or he hoped it was.

Galen paused. Then his voice lowered. 'Before we start, I have some news for you. Two months ago the boy and I came out of Tasceron, the Wounded City, the City of the Makers. While we were there we saw and heard things I couldn't explain if I wanted to. But this is the point. The Makers, at last, have spoken to the Order. They've sent us a message. They've promised us they will return.'

The silence was complete, as if no one breathed.

Then someone said, 'Is it certain?'

'I heard the voice myself, across space and time. The boy heard it, and others. They told us to wait.' He rubbed the edge of his hand wearily down his cheek. 'How long, I don't know. We must all pray it will be soon. Kest's creatures multiply, and the Unfinished Lands still spread. The Watch grows in strength. We need it to be soon.'

They were astonished. Their amazement was so strong Raffi felt he could almost have touched it; it was sharp as the holly hanging from the roof, bright as the berries the fire scorched. But they believed.

The keeper turned abruptly, ignoring the sudden buzz of whispers. 'Are your sense-lines out, boy? I may be too busy.'

Raffi nodded; he'd already checked them, a net of energy lines around the house, stretching out as far down the moonlit lanes and trackways as he could manage. If anyone crossed them, he'd know.

'Then we'll start,' Galen said.

He sat, waved a hand, and Raffi climbed to his feet, nervously waiting for the whispers to quieten.

Finally they were all looking at him.

He had only done this once before, though he had heard the story of Flain's death most years since he was small. Now he would recite it, from memory, from the Book of the Seven Moons. After that the keeper would enter the Silence, maybe for minutes, maybe for hours. Until he woke, like Flain had woken, bringing them the secret Word. And then the candles would be lit and, at last, they'd eat. Raffi was desperate for food. He'd been fasting all day, and now his stomach rumbled quietly. Gripping his fists, he began quickly.

'The soul that had been Flain travelled deep into the Otherworld, always seeking the way back. After hours and years and centuries he came to a low place, no higher from the floor than his knee, and he crawled among the veins and wormholes of the Underworld. Through the mines and tunnels of Death he crept, to a wide cavern lit only by red flame. In the centre of the cavern lay a casket, made of gold and calarna wood, and the soul of Flain crossed the soft sand to the casket and opened it.

'In the casket was a Word. And Flain saw the Word, and as he saw it all the secrets of the world came to him, and he knew the way out from Death, and the future; and far off and very faint, he heard the voices of the Makers – Tamar, Soren, Theriss – calling for him.'

Raffi stopped. In the silence the fire crackled,

smelling of pine and furzewood. Faces were red glimmers, sharp angles of shadow. As he sat down, all eyes turned to Galen.

The Relicmaster sat upright in his chair, his black hair glossy in the dimness, his eyes catching the flamelight. He sat easily, without moving, his face gaunt and calm. And as they watched, in the smoky hall, through the woodcrackle and the soft patter of hail on the shutters, they saw something begin to form, in the air before the fire.

A bench creaked, bodies leaned forward. A child said something and was hushed.

It came out of nowhere, out of the dark, and though they had all seen this happen before, the eerie chill of it was always new. Even Raffi felt the ice of fear touch his spine.

The casket was large, and strange, made of gold and calarna wood: Flain's casket, with its hinges gleaming. Slowly it became solid, until it was heavy, on a small table, the wood richly oiled.

Raffi stared. Every keeper made the casket differently; he had seen Galen perform the Flainsdeath summoning before, but never like this. It was so quick. Something was strange. Something was different.

Outside, the rising wind beat at the shutters. For a long moment Galen waited. Then he stood up, his hands on the lid.

'I open this,' he said, his voice hoarse and strange, 'as Flain did. Let the Word speak to us, let it teach us the secrets.'

It was back, the power that had possessed him before; the power that was the Crow. Dizzy with it, Raffi felt it crackle and rustle round the room like dark wings, making his fingers jerk and tingle, blurring some deep uneasy nagging in his head.

Now Galen was opening the lid, and as he lifted

11

it all the people gasped, because light came out of it, a widening slit, stabbing up into the smoke, throwing a brilliant glare on to Galen's face as he stared down into it, undazzled.

Raffi stood up. Something snagged in his mind, some warning. Outside, the wind howled and rattled.

With both hands, Galen was reaching eagerly into the casket. There were things he should have said, parts of the Litany. He wasn't saying them. Uneasy, Raffi shifted. 'Galen. The Responses.'

There was no sign he was heard.

'Galen?'

No one moved. Turning his head, Raffi saw why.

Shapes and swirls of energy were everywhere in the room, sparking up panelling, the folds of hangings, spitting along the tables. Amazed, the tenants stared around them. Small blue coils unwound, snapping back on themselves around Galen, leaving a faint smell of burning. Raffi had never seen anything like it before.

Then Galen spoke, abruptly. 'I see the Word!'

He lifted his eyes. They were black, as if blinded. Rocallion was standing; everyone was. A boy called out; there were noises from outside, horse hooves, running, a banging on the door. With a guilty shock Raffi dragged his mind back to the sense-lines; they were snagged open, torn wide.

'The Watch!' he hissed, but the keeper was rigid, the box in his hands pulsing with light.

'Would you hear the Word?'

'Speak it!' someone murmured, remembering the answer.

'I speak it.' Galen breathed sharply, as if a knife had stabbed him. 'The Word . . .' He sought for it, hands gripped tight, until suddenly his eyes cleared in shock. 'The word is . . . *Interrex*.'

The whole room stared at him in astonishment. Then the casket vanished, soundlessly.

Raffi moved. 'Rocallion, the Watch are here!' Shoving through the crowd he grabbed Galen's arm. 'They're here! At the door!'

'What!' The franklin stared at him in horror. 'But I've got men out.'

'They're through that! Listen!'

Voices were loud in the courtyard. A horse neighed, hooves clattered over the cobbles.

'Flainsteeth!' Rocallion leapt across the room and grabbed Galen. 'With me, keepers, now! Hurry!'

He dragged them through a door in the wall. Behind them Raffi could hear the table hastily dragged out, candles lit, the hurried children being pushed into seats. A Flainsnight supper was not illegal. Not yet.

They raced down a tiny stair, Raffi stumbling in the sudden dark. 'Your friends . . .' Galen gasped.

'Don't worry. They won't talk. Just a party.'

'Unless the Watch know we're here,' the keeper growled.

At the bottom was a corridor. Rocallion looked up and down it hastily, then opened a door opposite, hustled them through and bolted it behind him.

'Stillroom,' he hissed.

It was musky with herb smells, bunches of them hung from the ceiling. A bench was littered with glass phials and bowls. Someone was calling, far off in the house, but, ignoring it, Rocallion crouched and pulled a hidden catch near the hearth. Instantly a small panel slid open in the wall.

Galen crawled in, Raffi scrambling after him.

Rocallion's white face filled the gap. 'No one

else knows about this. I'll get you out when I can. You'll be safe.'

The keeper nodded. 'Good luck,' he said grimly. But the panel was slammed tight.

*Tamar dragged the thing before the
Council: a six-legged lizard, moaning in
pain, studded with spines.*

*'What abomination is this?' Flain
demanded.*

*'This lord, is what Kest has done in
secret.'*

And all eyes turned to me, in my corner.

Sorrows of Kest

They were crouched in some black, damp-smelling
place. Raffi stretched out his hand and touched a
cold wall.

'So.' Galen's voice came grimly out of the dark.
'They timed that well.'

'Will they find us?'

'It depends on how suspicious they are. Can you
see them?'

Raffi tried, opening the third eye, his mind's eye.
'Six?'

'More like ten.' Galen sounded distant, as if his
mind was listening to the uproar in the house.
'Hard to tell. There's a lot of confusion.' He must
have eased his leg then, because he hissed with
the ache of it; Raffi felt a faint echo of pain.

'Make a light, boy. Let's see where we are.'

It took Raffi an effort; concentrating made him
dizzy. But finally he managed a weak globe of light
in the air before him, wobbling.

'Hold it still!' Galen snapped, looking round.

They were in a tiny cell, hardly tall enough for

Galen to stand. The walls were damp brick – plastered once, but most of that lay in lumps on the floor. There were no windows. A crack in one corner let in an icy draught. In another corner was a basket, with a pile of blankets on top.

The globe faded. Raffi sweated with the effort of keeping it.

'Leave it.' Galen had the basket open, rummaging inside. A tinderbox sparked; Raffi saw the faint glow of kindling being blown red.

'Save your energy. We may be days in here.'

If we're lucky, Raffi thought. He let the globe go out. Then he asked 'Any food?'

'Some. Rocallion seems to have been prepared.'

'Unless he knew they were coming.'

Galen looked up sharply, his face dark. 'You think so?'

Raffi shrugged. 'No.'

'In that case, keep quiet, and don't slur a good man. Take the blankets. They're damp, but thick.'

Raffi tugged one round himself and shivered. Galen handed him bread, an apple, some strips of dried meat. 'Flainsnight feast,' he said.

Raffi stared at it in disgust. Then he ate. He was used to being hungry. Any food was something.

'We have enough for about two days.' Galen crunched an apple absently.

'Will it be that long?'

The keeper shrugged. 'If the leaf-fall is too thick the Watch will stay in the house.'

'He could bring us food.'

'He'll be followed. Everywhere.' Stretching his legs out, Galen considered. 'If no one else knows about this hiding-place we're dependent on him. At least his house-men can't betray us. If he has – ' He stopped, instantly. His hand shot to his neck.

'Oh God!' he hissed.

'What?' Raffi knelt up. 'What is it?'

Galen had flung the apple down, was searching his pockets, inside his jerkin, desperately. 'The beads! The awen-beads!'

They stared at each other in blank horror.

'Did you pick them up?'

'No. I . . .'

'God! Raffi!' Galen slammed one hand furiously against the wall.

'There are other things too,' Raffi realised miserably. 'Your stick. Our bags.'

'Those are well hidden. The beads were there – in that room!'

Guilty, sick with fear, Raffi sat rigid, seeing the strings of jet and green crystals in their interlocking circles. He should have grabbed them! He should have remembered them!

'I'm sorry,' he breathed.

Galen turned on him sourly. 'I suppose I should beat you black and blue.'

'No room,' he joked feebly.

'Nor any need. The Watch will do it for me.'

In the silence each of them imagined a gloved hand snatching up the beads; a yell. Any Watchman would recognize them at once.

'Maybe one of the tenants found them.'

'Listen!' Galen caught him.

Footsteps ran down the stairs above, loud heavy boots. Galen snuffed the candle instantly. The still-room door banged open. Someone came in and paced around.

They know, Raffi thought. His hands clenched, he huddled in the dark.

They were searching. Cups crashed over. Something made of glass fell and shattered. A foot kicked impatiently along the panelling.

It'll sound hollow, he thought, clutching his arms

as if he could make himself smaller. Galen was a still shadow against the wall.

It did sound hollow, but the searcher seemed not to notice. Someone called him; he yelled back, 'Down here,' in a voice so close it made Raffi sweat. Then he was pounding up the stairs again, the door banging behind him.

Silence. A long silence.

Finally, tight with terror, Raffi made himself uncurl. He drew a deep ragged breath.

'Sit still,' Galen said sourly. 'They'll be back.'

They were. All evening, late into the night, the house was alive with bangs and shouts, thudding doors and footsteps. Every time Raffi finally dozed into uneasy sleep under the mothy blanket, some crash or voice jerked him awake, cold with sweat, his hands clenched. He was sick and giddy with fear. Galen never spoke, perhaps didn't even hear. He stayed where he was, knees drawn up, quite still in the dark. Raffi knew he was deep in prayer, lost in a rigid meditation, and how the keeper had the discipline for it astonished him. Once or twice he tried himself, gabbling the Litany and the Appeal to Flain, but the words dried up, or he found himself repeating one phrase foolishly over and over, all his attention fixed on the clatter round the house.

Not knowing was the worst.

Had they found the beads? Were they tearing the place apart? Was Rocallion under torture? Had he talked? When would the smoke start curling under the panel, choking them, driving them out into the swords and crossbows of the Watch?

He tossed and curled and uncurled hopelessly until, without even realising he'd been asleep, he was awake, staring at the crack of cold daylight, the sudden sharp stink of a midden somewhere.

He rolled over and sat up.

Gaunt in the dark, Galen was watching. After a moment he said, 'Take something to eat. One swallow of water from the jar.'

'Have you . . .?'

'Hours ago.'

Guiltily, Raffi broke a stiffening crust and ate it, with a tiny piece of cheese. The water was cool and fresh; he tried not to take a big swallow. 'Did you sleep?'

Galen glared, the grim look Raffi loathed. 'I prayed for forgiveness. So should you.'

'I don't – '

'The beads, boy!' Galen shook his head in disgust. 'I let myself fear – I forgot that the Makers have us all in their hands! We have to trust them. They won't let the Watch find us unless they wish it, and if they do, so be it. Who are we to be afraid.'

Raffi chewed the bread. 'It's hard not to be.'

'You're a scholar. I'm a master and should know better.'

Galen was always harsh; harshest of all with himself. That moment of terror would irritate him; it would be a long time before he would forgive himself for it. Raffi sat back, thinking of the Crow, the strange power of the Makers' messenger that had entered Galen in Tasceron, filling him with unknown abilities. Since then there had been little sign of it. Galen had been normal – grim, short-tempered, fierce. Until last night. Raffi licked the last crumbs from his fingers. Last night, it had come back. In a whisper he asked, 'What happened, at the Summoning?'

Galen raised dark eyes. Dragging the long hair from his neck, he knotted it in a piece of string.

19

Then he said, 'I'm not sure. The casket ... I made the casket as I always do, but when it came, it was different. Bigger. Then the light ... if I made that I don't know how. And I've never felt a word so surely. It burned through me like fire.' He glanced up. 'Did I say it aloud?'

'Yes. You said "Interrex".'

Galen scowled. 'Maybe the Watch should have come sooner. Some messages are not for everyone to hear.'

'Don't joke about the Watch.' Raffi wriggled under the blanket. 'What does it mean?'

'Interrex? It's a word from the Apocalypse. It means one who rules between the kings.'

'But what ...?'

'Enough questions!' Galen sat upright, abruptly. 'If we're going to be cooped up in here we'll use the time. I've neglected your studies, so first we go over the Sorrows of Kest. From the beginning.'

It was an endless day.

Galen drilled him in every chapter of the Sorrows; then they worked through the Litany, the Book of the Seven Moons, the Sayings of the Archkeepers, even the eternal life of Askelon with its forty-seven Prophecies of the Owl. He learned the last twenty wearily, repeating them after Galen in a whisper, the keeper impatiently correcting.

They dared not speak aloud; four times someone came into the stillroom. Once, an animal – a dog, Raffi thought – scratched at the panel, but Galen made a thought-flare that sent it squealing. Each time Galen went back to work, grimly. Raffi knew it was just to keep them both busy, to stop the fear, but in the end it was agony; all he wanted to do was scream. By the time the keeper let him rest, his voice cracking with thirst, the daylight in the corner was long gone. So was most of the food.

Raffi took an agonisingly small sip of water. 'He must come tonight. He won't let us starve in here.'

'Maybe.' Galen slumped against the wall. 'Maybe not.'

Pulling himself up awkwardly, Raffi limped about. He was stiff with the cold, a bitter cold that felt like snow. Bending down, he tried to see out, but the crack was too narrow. He jammed a rag into it, and instantly felt Galen's hand grab him; a warning grip.

The panel was sliding open.

The candle guttered. When the flame steadied they saw Rocallion crawling in. He looked tired and haggard, tugging food and another jar of water from under his jerkin. 'Eat this,' he gasped. 'Quickly. I've got to get you out.'

Galen caught hold of him. 'Did they find the beads?'

'What beads?' Then his eyes widened. 'Have you lost them?'

'We left them in the room.'

The young man rubbed his hair frantically. 'I don't know! The fat man hasn't mentioned them!'

'Then they're safe. One of your friends must have them.' Galen sat back in relief. 'How did you get away?'

'Don't ask.'

Stuffing bread into his mouth, Raffi muttered, 'How many of them are there?'

'A full patrol. They've searched the house, questioned everyone. I hope it was just a random visit.'

'No one gave anything away?'

Rocallion looked strained. 'No. But they –' Instantly, he stopped.

Raffi swallowed hard.

Outside, in the stillroom, something had shifted. A tiny movement, a creak of floorboard, but they all knew what it meant. Someone had followed him.

Rocallion closed his eyes in despair. He almost spoke, but Galen shook his head fiercely, snuffing the candle with one swift jab. Raffi felt the power gather in him, in the darkness around them.

Slowly, the panel opened.

Someone stood there, shadowy. Then the figure crouched, and to Raffi's astonishment, a small hand stretched into the cell, and he caught the glint of the green and black beads that swung from its fingers.

'You know, you shouldn't leave these things lying around, Galen,' a voice said, amused. 'Anyone might find them.'

3

Between the kings the Interrex shall come;
come from the dark and to the darkness
go.

Apocalypse of Tamar

'Carys!'

The girl grinned at them in the dimness. 'Hello,
Raffi. Still hungry?'

'You know her?' Rocallion was staring in astonishment. 'But she's one of the Watch!'

'Her name is Carys Arrin. As for what she is,
only God and the Makers know.' In the half-light
Galen reached out gently and took the beads from
her fingers. 'So it was you who found them.'

'Luckily for you.' She glanced back at the door.
'But we haven't got time to talk. The Watch com-
mander is called Braylwin. He's fat and lazy, but
he's got a mind like a razor and he's sure there
was a keeper here for Flainsnight. I'm not exactly
the apple of his eye, either. So I want you out of
here.'

'You think we'd betray you?' Galen said, quietly.

'Under torture, yes.' She stared hard at him, her
short brown hair swinging. 'Look, I can get you
out if you come now. I'm guard leader for two
hours, and everything's quiet. The patrol will stay
here at least a week, Galen. You might not get
another chance.'

Galen blessed the beads, pulled them on, then
stiffly crawled out of the cell and stood up. 'Of
course we trust you,' he said, as if she'd asked.

Bewildered, Rocallion stared up at him. 'Are you sure?'

Raffi grinned. 'We think so.'

'Think!'

'Hope.'

Carys was already at the door, peering round it. In the darkness she seemed taller, her hair shorter. The crossbow was slung at her back. She said, 'We go down the corridor, then the cellar stairs. Can the cellar door be opened from inside?'

Rocallion shrugged. 'The Watch have got the keys.'

'I've got the keys. There's a guard in the court-yard; I'll talk to them while you get by. Down the lane is a byre, by the gate – it's been searched already. We'll meet there. Agreed?'

She's used to giving orders, Raffi thought.

Galen nodded. It was hard to see his expression in the dimness. Glancing back, she said suddenly, 'Make sure you wait for me, Galen, because I've got something to tell you. Something important.'

As he stepped forward into the lamplight from the corridor, they caught his wolfish smile. 'I know that.'

'You would!' For a moment she grinned back. Then she was out of the door. Galen pushed Raffi after her, then came himself, with Rocallion silently at the back.

The corridor was empty, lit with one lamp. Far off in the house someone laughed. They clustered at the end while Rocallion took his keys from Carys and fumbled for the right one; as soon as the door opened they slipped through.

It closed behind them with a click.

'Be careful,' Rocallion's voice echoed. 'There are steps in front of you leading down.'

Raffi found them, edging cautiously. He knew

they were in the cellar – it was bitterly cold and smelt of beercasks. Twice at the bottom he walked into barrels. Finally Rocallion pushed through from the back. 'Let me go first.'

There was no light and Galen made none; it would have been fatal if the door above had opened.

When Raffi caught up with Rocallion, the back door was already unlocked. Infinitely carefully, the franklin opened it and looked out. Under his arm Raffi saw the dim courtyard, dark gables, a single star overhead.

A murmur of talk came from somewhere near by. Carys pushed her way silently to the front. 'Take care,' she breathed. Then she squeezed past them and went out into the night.

They waited. Raffi felt the cold drift of the leaf-fall on his face, heard the hiss of it against the roofs of the manor-house. The night was unusually still, as if held in frost, though far off in the woods an owl called, and nearer something squeaked, like a jekkle-mouse.

The voices had gone. Instead only Carys was talking, loud and furious. He could hear the anger in her voice, and was amazed again at the way she could lie, and pretend, and act.

'Go now,' Galen whispered. They slid carefully out into the blue shadows, edging along the wall.

The leaf-drift had fallen all day. Here in the lee of the wall it was a bare sprinkling, so that their feet cut dark prints; Galen scuffed them out, hurriedly. They sprinted between buildings, under the low eaves of a barn. As they flitted through a gate, Raffi glimpsed the red glare of a fire, heard Carys's sharp orders. She wanted a sharper watch kept. And she wanted those dice! Now! Raffi grinned, his fingers slipping over the cold of the gate bar.

In the lane they could run, but the ruts were full of frosted puddles that tilted and splintered, wheezing as they broke. The ground was rock hard and even the firethorns had leaf-dust all over them; the storm had brought a sudden sharp frost, the first this year. Raffi shivered, his breath smoking in the sudden glint of two moons that drifted from the clouds.

Galen pulled him into the hedge-shadow. 'This byre. How far?'

Rocallion caught his breath. 'Just ahead.'

They could see the low edge of its roof, among branches. This end of the lane was banked with leaves; a great wall, well-trampled, as if cows had forced a way through. The pungent smell of fireberries was rank.

Rocallion put his hands on the door-bar, but Galen stopped him. 'Wait.'

In silence the keeper stood, one hand on the wall. They both knew he was sending sense-lines inside.

'I thought you trusted her?' Rocallion whispered.

'We do. And we don't.'

Then the keeper nodded, and they lifted the bar and hurried in. The byre was empty, deep with old straw. A rat rustled away. Breathless, they crouched in the cold; Raffi buried himself in straw.

'Maybe I should go back,' Rocallion murmured.

As he said it the door creaked; Carys slipped in and stood there. She folded her arms and grinned at them. 'I'm glad you stayed.'

'I wouldn't have missed it,' Galen said gravely. 'But won't they miss you?'

She came over and sat by them, taking the crossbow off and tossing it down. 'Them! They'll be glad to see the back of me.' She hugged her knees. 'So what have you both been doing? How did you get out of the city?'

'The Sekoi have ways,' Galen said carelessly. 'After that the three of us came north and paid a little visit to a thief-lord named Alberic.'

She laughed. 'We know about that. He's after you.'

'Is he?' Raffi was alarmed.

'Some of our spies have reported that he's sent men out, asking questions. You should be careful.'

'I intend to be,' Galen said drily. 'Did you hear how Raffi climbed up the wall of his tower?'

She giggled. 'I didn't think you had it in you.'

'Neither did I,' Raffi muttered, remembering the terror of the swinging rope, his raw hands.

Carys was silent a moment. Then she looked up, her eyes bright. 'I've got some information you'll find ... interesting. It's highly secret.' Her glance flickered to Rocallion.

He caught it, and stood up. 'Your packs are hidden in an old well out near here. I'll get them for you.'

When he had gone she got up and checked the door, then came back and crouched. Excitement was streaming from her; Raffi could almost see it, and he struggled up in the straw, his skin tingling.

'Listen,' she said. 'Last month, up in the hills, an old woman was being questioned.'

'Questioned?' Galen looked at her grimly.

'I can't help their methods. In any case, she suddenly came out with some amazing information, probably to save herself. She told them she once worked in the Emperor's palace. When the Emperor was killed at the fall of Tasceron, the young man next to him, whose body was too badly burned to be sure about, was assumed to have been his son. According to the old woman, this

wasn't so. The son, the Prince, escaped. He lived
for many years in hiding in a village named Carno.
He married, and seven years ago he had a child.
The old woman lived with them. Her name was
Marta. No one else knew who they were. But then
a Watch patrol came for slave labourers for the
mines at Far Reach. They took the parents, and
the old woman, though she was no good to them.
No one seems to know what happened to the
child.'

'And the Prince?' Galen muttered.

'Dead. We checked.'

They were silent. Then Raffi breathed out
slowly. 'So the Emperor had a grandchild.'

Galen pondered, his eyes glinting. 'This is excel-
lent news, Carys, if it's true . . . Boy or girl?'

'That was one thing she wouldn't say.'

'A new Emperor!' Galen stood up and limped
around in excitement. 'It's a miracle! And it fits.
When the Makers come back everything will be
restored.'

'You're still sure they're coming?' Carys asked
quietly.

'You were there. You heard them.'

She shook her head, rueful. 'I heard something.
A voice. But look, Galen, if you want this Interrex
of yours – '

'What did you say?' The keeper whirled round,
staring at her, his eyes black. In the shadows his
face was suddenly hooked and sharp. The Crow's
face.

'I said Interrex. It's Braylwin's joke. It's from
your Book.'

He glanced at Raffi. 'Once again.'

Carys frowned. 'What do you mean, again?'

'It was the Word. On Flainsnight. The word the
Makers sent.'

28

For a moment she looked at Galen, so still and strangely that he felt something flame up in her, some doubt or anger. Then she said bleakly, 'Well, anyway, if you want this Interrex you'd better find him fast. Or her. Because we're already looking.'

'We?'

'The Watch. And the reward is big, believe me.'

Galen came close to her, suddenly. 'Leave the Watch, Carys! Come with us.'

'I've told you I won't. You could be all wrong, Galen. Mistaken about everything.'

He smiled, coldly. 'Was the Crow wrong? When you saw the House of Trees break into leaf, when you heard a voice from the stars, was all that a mistake? You know it wasn't.'

The silence was bitter.

Then, abruptly, the door banged open and Rocallion backed in, two packs in his arms and Galen's stick thrust through his belt. A gust of leaf-dust swirled in with him.

Carys stood up. 'I've told you. You must do what you want about it. If the Watch find the child they'll kill it, that's for sure.' Then she laughed at them, eyes bright. 'I'm not really with the Watch, Galen. I'm for myself, I told you that. There are things I want to find out, and being on the inside is the best way. Braylwin's lazy; he spends every winter in the Tower of Song, and I want to go with him, because that's where all the Watch records are kept. I need to know who I am. Where I came from. But you must find the Interrex. That word was for you.'

She was at the door but she stopped when Raffi blurted out, 'You haven't told us how you've been.'

'Under suspicion.' She kicked the straw absently. 'I put in a report about Tasceron. It was a master-piece of lies – you'd have loved it, Raffi. But someone must guess I'm holding back. I was hauled off surveillance and assigned to this Braylwin. For the time being I'm stuck with him. He's as sly as they come. And odious.'

'Be careful,' Raffi muttered.

She nodded.

Galen gave Rocallion a hurried blessing; the young man knelt hastily in the straw.

'Go back with her,' he told him. Then turning to Carys, he said, 'Get him into the house. I don't want him in any trouble for this, Carys. He's done nothing but save our lives.'

'Don't worry.'

Rocallion shook Galen's hand, then Raffi's. 'Good luck, keepers,' he said.

'And you,' Galen answered. 'Both of you.'

From the door Carys gave them a strange look. 'I'll survive. But if you find this child, Galen, will you let me know? Will you trust me enough to tell me where it is? You'll need the Watch kept away.'

For a moment he stared at her darkly. Then he said, 'You'll hear from me, Carys.'

4

It is impossible for the agent to be over-cunning, or have too little conscience.

Rule of the Watch

Braylwin poured half a flaskful of Rocallion's best wine into a glass and sipped it, licking every drop from his lips. As Carys came in, his hand hovered over the dish of spiced chicken, picking out a succulent piece.

'Well?'

She went over to the fire and stared down angrily into the flames, leaning her forehead on the chimney-piece. 'You're scum, Braylwin. Odious, stinking scum.'

He smiled an oily smile. 'Ah, poor Carys. How hard she takes it! And not even to have any reward at the end of it – because all that will be mine. Anyway, it was your idea.' He spat a bone elegantly to one side and mopped his lips. 'Tell uncle all about it.'

'Galen's gone. And the boy.'

'You got them past the guard?'

'Only too easily.'

'And they had no idea I knew about them? None at all, Carys?'

She twisted, glaring at him. 'Not from me. But Galen's . . . well, he's got ways of knowing. I can't be sure.'

'Mmm. Well, it will have to do. Because if I thought you were playing your little tricks on me,

31

sweetie, your uncle would be annoyed. Very annoyed.'

She hated him. At that moment, staring down at his sleek skullcap, she longed to put a crossbow bolt through him, and was shocked at herself. Gripping her fists, she kept her voice calm. 'I told them about the Interrex – all the information we had. I'm not sure it'll work. He won't know where to look any more than you.'

'He won't. But keepers have ways of finding things out. It's said they talk to trees.' He giggled.

'As a matter of fact,' she said, savagely, 'they do.'

The small sharp eyes fixed on her. 'Ah, I'd forgotten you know all about them. One day, Carys, I'll find out exactly what did go on in Tasceron.' He scratched his cheek and selected another piece of meat. She watched him, cold with fury, his fur-trimmed coat and the tiny black skullcap he wore to keep warm. 'They'll find the Interrex for us. What keeper could resist it?' He licked his thumb. 'And as you say, it saves us doing any of the work. We get them, and the child, and a nice fat sack of gold. Or at least I do. Probably promotion too.'

'What about me?'

He wagged a greasy finger at her. 'You get away with your life, sweetheart. And uncle doesn't tell about that business at Carner's Haven.'

She turned back to the fire, knowing he was smirking behind her. 'Galen is worth ten of you,' she snarled.

'He is, is he? That remark is enough to get you two years patrolling ice. Or worse. If you play games with the Watch, Carys, you pay the price.' She heard him clink his glass thoughtfully. 'Does it hurt so much to betray them – the keeper, the boy, the cat-creature? Perhaps it does. Long ago I might have felt the same.'

'I doubt it.'

He glanced over. 'High and mighty. But underneath, you and I are just the same, Carys.'

Suddenly her disgust was too much. She turned and stalked past him, slamming the door, pushing two of Rocallion's housegirls aside. Upstairs, in the small room she'd taken for herself, she flung the crossbow down and herself after it, on to the bed.

How could she have brought herself to this? Been so stupid?

Rolling over she stared up at the ceiling, thinking back to Carner's Haven.

It had been the first time she'd seen the Watch take children, and it had shaken her. The patrol had ridden down to the village early, Braylwin on his new green-painted horse, but somehow the villagers had had warning. The place was in total confusion. All the children under ten were in hiding; the men yelling threats and the women screeching with anger and fear. 'Search the place!' he'd roared, and she'd been the one to go into the barn in the last field and see the little girl wriggling halfway out of the straw.

Thumping the mattress, Carys got up and went to the window, tugging it open. Leaf-dust drifted against her lips.

Carefully, she remembered that moment. The girl had been about four or five, crying, her face contorted with terror. The mother had burst out of hiding between them.

'For God's sake,' she'd breathed, 'Let her go! Let us go!'

It was only then Carys had realized the crossbow had been loaded and aimed; she'd lowered it abruptly, astonished.

Why had she let them escape? Even now she wasn't sure. Was it that the little girl with the brown hair might have been herself, all those years ago? Had she cried when the Watch took her? She couldn't remember. She couldn't remember her mother or father, her village, anything before the grim stone rooms and snowy courtyards of Watchtower 547, Marn Mountain. Maybe that was why she'd lifted the baby and pushed her hurriedly through a gap in the back wall to the mother outside. Thinking about it made her feel uneasy, even now. Galen would have been pleased. Why did it matter what Galen thought?

She looked unhappily up for the moons but they were lost behind cloud; pale strange edges and nebulous glimmers. It would have been all right, but when she had turned round Braylwin had been standing inside the barn door, looking at her. He'd seen enough; she'd known instantly that he would use it against her. All he'd said was, 'Oh, sweetheart!' in that mock-surprised, stupid way he had. But he'd seen.

All he had to do was report it.

Things were tricky enough already. They'd certainly have her in for questioning, and she knew too much. The House of Trees, the Order's safe house in Tasceron, that Galen was the Crow, they'd get all that out of her – she dared not let them question her. Moodily she stared at the windowsill and cursed Galen to the Pit for letting her remember it all. Braylwin had her in his power, and how he loved it. Carys do this, Carys do that, all the worst work, the wretched endless reports. She was sick of it.

And then he had found the awen-beads.

His fat hand had picked them delicately from around the candles and she'd recognized them with a cold stab of dread. She knew Braylwin would tear the house apart to find a keeper. It had been her plan to let Raffi and Galen go and urge them to find the Interrex – the only thing she could think of on the spot.

But Braylwin had liked it. It was clever, and meant no work for him. He was lazy. That was one weakness she could use.

Perhaps she should have told Galen. Warned him. Or maybe not. He had to find this child in any case, and when he did ... well, she'd worry about that when it happened. At least they were free.

Out in the cold night Agramon loomed suddenly from behind cloud, outlining the dusty buildings and the fields beyond, their hedgerows dark and spiny, the trees branching against pale sky.

It had been good to see them both again. Raffi looked a bit taller. Where were they now, she wondered, out in that leaf-littered land? Where would they go?

For a brief, bitter second she wished she was with them, that she was walking down the muddy lanes away from here, away from the Watch, laughing with Raffi. Then, fiercely, she banged the window shut and turned her back on it.

Braylwin was going to the Tower of Song.

And she was going with him.

Games of Chance

5

Flain's anger made the sky shudder. Stars fell; the new seas boiled.

Before them all, Kest swore he would make no more creatures; he abjured his poisons and philtres and alchemies. But his heart was full of resentment. And he lied.

Book of the Seven Moons

The hedgerows were ripe with berries, swelling russet and red in the long five-month autumn of Anara. As he walked, Raffi picked handfuls, eating some and tossing the rest into a small sack on his back. Far ahead, Galen leaned impatiently on a field-gate.

Tall fireweed blazed scarlet; the leaves of hawthorn and elder and strail clogged the ruts, and from somewhere not far off the smell of smoke drifted – a stubble field burning, or from the chimney of a house. Raffi pulled a maggot from a fat blackberry and tossed it aside, into a patch of withering white-lady that glinted with dew.

'Come on, boy,' Galen growled.

They were two days' walk from Rocallion's manor, and deep in the network of tracks and lanes called the Meres. This was flat, marshy country, wet underfoot, the rich grasses sprouting from saturated peat. All day the two of them had squelched through it; Galen morose, brooding, striding relentlessly for hours and then sitting silent while the mists and fen fogs gathered round him.

Picking a last berry, Raffi walked down the lane. The day was waning. Fog was thickening on the fields; in a copse on the horizon, woses chattered. Galen stared out grimly at the wood. 'Hear it?'

Raffi nodded, bitterly. He'd hoped they'd spend the night under those trees, but not now. Woses were filthy and noisy, and savage in packs.

'We'll keep moving,' the keeper muttered.

The fog gathered, swirling out of ditches and dykes. As they trudged on further it closed in, and they lost sight of what was behind, pushing through a rich bruised smell of berries and hawthorn, the wet branches swinging back into their faces, stumbling in hidden ruts and puddles.

Halfway up a long slow climb, Galen stopped. He turned his head. 'Listen.'

Glad of a rest, Raffi hitched his pack up, breathing hard. A bat squeaked in the twilight just above him.

And then he heard it: the slow, wet clopping of a horse's hooves. It was behind them, coming up the hill.

Galen turned, the drops of fen fog glinting in his black hair. On each side the hedge was dim, spiny, unbreakable.

'Quick!' he breathed.

They climbed hastily up through the mist, moving in a strange luminous greyness. One of the moons must be out – Cyrax, perhaps – and her pearl-pale shimmer blurred the haze.

As he hurried, Raffi sent a sense-line back, feeling instantly the hot breath of the horse, the sweaty strength of it, the heaviness of its rider.

Then Galen grabbed his arm, tugging him into the fog. Bushes loomed up and at their base a hole, wormed by some animal. Even as he fell on his stomach and wriggled in, Raffi knew they were taking a risk, and he tore his coat recklessly off the thorns. The hedge cracked and snapped; he breathed prayers of silence at it, apologies, feeling the trees' reluctant, displeased hush.

With a hiss of pain Galen was in too. He raised his hand and Raffi saw, with a shiver of fear, that a Kest-claw clung to him. Galen flung it off and stamped on it, over and over. Blood ran between his fingers.

'It's bitten you!'

'I'll live,' Galen muttered. 'I've had it before.' But Raffi knew this was bad. A Kest-claw bit deep, poisoning the blood, sending dizziness and sickness, sometimes for days. It could kill.

Galen wrapped the wound tight, crouching.

Hooves thumped close on the track. From here, deep in leaves, his ear next to the ground, Raffi felt the heavy thump in his head like a pulse. Harness jangled. The horse blew and whickered and a man coughed, a deep bark.

Carefully, Raffi parted the leaves. He saw the horse's legs. It had stopped.

There was no doubt it could smell them both, hear them too. Galen was still; Raffi knew he had sent a thought-line out to the beast, was soothing it, speaking words of comfort to it. Inching to one side, he saw the rider.

A man, muffled in coats and a hood. Difficult to see; a misty figure, its head turning to look round, until a wraith of fog drifted away and the moon glimmered suddenly on armour, a heavy crossbow.

The man turned. Raffi glimpsed eyes, beard, wet hair.

Then he muttered something, and the horse clopped on, vanishing strangely into the mist.

For a long time they crouched still, hearing it

toil up the invisible hill, until the harness creak faded into silence, and only the smell of its droppings hung on the air.

Galen leaned back. 'Well, well.'

'What?'

'Didn't you recognize him?'

Raffi scrambled round. 'No. Who?'

'Godric. Remember him? One of Alberic's men.'

A drop of dew slid into Raffi's ear; chilled, he shook it out. 'Alberic!'

'Who else?' Galen eased his legs out, flattening nettles. 'I'm not that surprised. Carys warned us. And when a thief-lord screams out that he'll kill you, he usually means it. He must have men out on all the roads. They'll ask in every village too. We'll have to go twice as carefully. And we'll have to get to the Sekoi before they do.'

'How far to the meeting place?' Raffi asked anxiously.

'About a day. We'll spend a few hours here and travel on before dawn. You can get the food out.'

Raffi nodded, unhappy. 'But what about your hand?'

The keeper glared at him. 'Leave that to me.'

As Raffi pulled some dried fish from the pack and ate it, Galen worked. He took leaves from the pocket at his waist: salve-all, Flainsglove, agrimony. Some he chewed, others he steeped carefully in cold water, binding them tight against his palm. The water should have been hot, Raffi knew. 'Look,' he said 'we could make a fire. The fog will hide it.'

'No time. A few hours' sleep, that's all. Then I'll wake you.'

Raffi lay down. It was useless to argue. Carys might have tried, but he knew better. There was something in Galen that was dark, untouchable: a grimness that all the unhappiness of his life had bred – the destruction of the Order, his hatred of the Watch. 'A driven man,' the Sekoi had remarked once, and Raffi knew what it meant. And since Tasceron, since the Crow had possessed him, it was stronger.

He began the night prayer wearily and fell asleep in the middle of it.

When he woke he was stiff and cold and damp. It was still dark. Nettle-rash itched all down his cheek.

Galen was gone.

Instantly, Raffi was alert. He sent sense-lines sprawling and touched the keeper, close, scrambling out of the hole anxiously. In the lane it was deep midnight. The mist had gone; huge and still over the black land hung six of the great moons – Atelgar, Agramon, Pyra, Karnos, craggy Lar, distant Atterix. Two were full, the rest fingernails and crescents of pink and blue and pearl.

Galen was standing in the blended light, his arms folded, staring up. As Raffi splashed a puddle he turned, and for a second there was something other in him that looked out, sharpening the blackness of his eyes, his long glossy hair, the muddy coat.

Then it was just Galen.

Raffi swung his pack on, reluctantly.

'Slept enough?' The keeper strode off without waiting for an answer, down the moonlit track. 'Sleeping and eating, boy. All you're good for.' He swung his stick down from his back. 'Now we step out. We're meeting the Sekoi at Tastarn, and we need to get there fast.'

'Then what?'

Galen looked at him sidelong. 'Then the Interrex.'

'Where do we start looking?'

Galen laughed, that sudden laugh that always turned Raffi cold. 'You'll be surprised,' he muttered.

All the rest of that night, as the moons swung slowly above them, they walked, silent; out of the dark and into the morning, the sun breaking through infinite veils of haze out of the watery fens. Herons rose and flapped; acres of bleak rushes moved and stirred, their seed rising in clouds. The long track led down into hollows and marshy swamps, through endless plantations of spindly willow, and as the sun rose so did the midges, biting and stinging.

At midday, worn and thirsty, they stopped. Galen was sweating, his coat hanging open, and as he ate Raffi took a sideways look at him. The keeper was ashen, dark hair plastered to his forehead. The Kest-claw's venom was working in him.

'You should rest.'

Galen rubbed his face with the back of his hand. 'Two hours from here,' he said hoarsely, 'is Tastarn. I'll rest there.'

But they went slower, all afternoon. It grew warm, even sultry; far off in the hills thunder growled and cracked. Galen stumbled, as if the energy of it had struck him like a wave. They left the track and crossed a stream, keeping east, through woods of delicate silver sheshorn trees that threshed in the faintest stirring of air. Munching berries, Raffi watched Galen anxiously, but the keeper walked fiercely, relentlessly. It was only when the roofs of Tastarn rose up among the trees

44

that he staggered, crumpling aganst a great oak by the track.

Raffi raced up. 'Sit down!' he said. 'Take a rest.'

Galen slid down the tree till he was sitting, and leaned his head back. He looked grey; his hands shook as he dragged the waterflask to his lips, then poured it over his face.

Raffi crouched next to him. 'Listen. You can't go into the village, not like this. It's not safe! We could both be caught too easily.'

The keeper shivered. 'Are you trying to give me advice?' he snapped.

'Yes. Stay here. I'll go in and fetch the Sekoi. He'll be easy to find.'

There was silence. A soft warm rain began to fall on them, pattering lightly on the leaves overhead. Galen dragged his hair back. Raffi knew he was struggling to think; the fever was confusing him.

'I won't be long. You've got plenty of water. You could sleep.'

'I don't need sleep.'

'Well, rest. Can you manage some sense-lines?'

Galen glared at him. 'Just about.'

'And you'd have the box.' The box was the relic, the light-weapon of the Makers they'd stolen back from Alberic. Since then neither of them had used it. The dwarf might have emptied it of power, Raffi thought suddenly. But no. He wanted it back.

Sweat or rain ran down Galen's chin. 'All right,' he hissed at last. 'All right. But be back by dark, Raffi, or I'm coming in to find you.'

Nodding, Raffi slipped off the pack and pushed it into the bracken.

'Wait,' Galen muttered. 'Leave your beads.'

For a moment Raffi hesitated; then he slipped off his two threads of blue and purple beads and put them in the keeper's hot hand. Without them he felt strange; as if some protection had gone. But Galen was right. It would be safer.

He stood up. 'Will you be all right?'

Galen glared at him, furious. Then he said, 'Nightfall. Remember.'

With a grin Raffi turned and ran down the track into the soft rain, and only when he got down to the stream did he glance back.

Galen was gone. Only a quivering of branches showed where he'd moved. For a moment Raffi felt guilty, leaving him, but there was no choice. And it should be easy to find the Sekoi.

Oddly happy, he jumped the stream and crossed a field of sheep, climbing a wall into a narrow road. Small houses loomed out of the rain, a goat chewing thoughtfully outside the nearest.

He walked, warily, into the village. It was busy. A small market was going on in the main street; he heard and smelt it even before he turned the corner. Pens of squalling hens and slow black cattle bellowing their discomfort; men standing around a great bull; stalls of hot bread and cooked meats, clothes, garish rings and belts. He wished he had some money, just to buy something. Not wanting to speak to anyone he wandered round, hands in pockets, watching carefully. Above the market-place rose the ominous black Watchtower; he could see men on its roof. A group of them moved through the market too, wearing the usual dark motley of worn armour, whips tied around their waists. The crowd opened for them, no one looked round.

Raffi backed away, behind a food stall. An old man was there, his arm deep in a barrel pulling out apples.

Raffi decided to take a risk. 'I'm looking for a

Sekoi,' he said quietly. 'Tall. Brindled, a zigzag under one eye. Have you seen it?'

'Seen it!' the old man grunted, straightening. He looked at Raffi curiously. 'It's been cleaning everyone out for days. In Marcy's, it'll be.'

'Marcy's?'

The old man wheezed. Then he turned Raffi round and pointed. 'Marcy's, son. Not for the likes of you.'

It was a low, squalid building, the roof patched and the windows all but smothered in ivy. One dim door hung open; even from here he could smell the stink of the place.

'Take my advice.' The old man leaned back into the barrel. 'Keep your hand on your money.'

'Thanks,' Raffi muttered.

Squeezing between cattle, pigs, jugglers, sausage-sellers, he made his way up to the broken hanging shutter of a window, and peered in.

The room was smoky; fires burned there, and lamps were lit. It was crammed with men, a noisy, jostling, uproarious crowd. In the middle was a table and round it some players were gambling at cards. Large piles of gold coins were stacked in front of them. Three of the players Raffi could see, the other was hidden by the passing crowd.

Then he ducked back with a sudden indrawn breath.

The horseman, Godric, was standing by the hearth. He had a grey tankard in his hand, its lid open, and he was drinking from it now, his eyes fixed on the card game.

Someone laughed. Men moved away.

And through the gap Raffi saw the fourth player, chatting and shuffling the cards with its seven fingers, a great stack of yellow gold heaped in front of it.

It was the Sekoi.
And Alberic's man was watching its back.

6

I watched him, day by day.
Suspicious, I followed his eyes,
the movements of his hands.
I knew my brother plotted.
What his plan was I could never see.

Apocalypse of Tamar

Crouching under the tangle of ivy, Raffi watched the smoky room in despair. How could he warn the Sekoi?

The creature was enjoying itself. Its seven long fingers rippled the cards expertly, flicking them out into rapid fans and shuffles. It was laughing, its yellow eyes bright as the gold stacked in front of it, the fur on its sharp face tense with excitement.

Carefully, Raffi rustled the ivy. No one even looked. He glanced at Godric; the man had his great scarf open, showing his black stiff beard and the glint of the rusty breastplate. He had found somewhere to sit – the end of a bench full of bargaining market-men – and he leaned back there, a threatening shadow, his eyes always on the Sekoi's back.

It was hopeless.

Raffi turned away and stared out into the rain. What would Galen do?

Pray.

The answer came at once as if someone had said it, and he nodded, sending his mind out in the long call to the Makers: to Flain the Tall, Soren, Lady of Leaves, Tamar, Beast-bringer, Theriss, Halen. Surely one of them could send him some idea.

He turned back, rain dripping on him from the tattered thatch. The Sekoi's fingers whisked in a few more coins. The other players looked disgusted. The shadow that was Godric drank in silence.

He would have to try some sort of Rapport. It was probably too hard for him. And it meant going inside.

Desperate now, he went round to the door and cautiously edged down three steps into the noise. The stench and smoke made him cough: a smell of beer and bodies and sizzling food. Before he even began he knew he couldn't do it. There were too many people shoving him, too much shouting and laughing. Someone grabbed his arm; he turned in fear and saw a woman, her face painted green and blue, holding him with sharp nails.

'Lost, darling?' she simpered, her voice slurred. 'You're not Tomas, are you? Tomas looks like you.'

He tugged away and ran, pushing through the crowd, fighting his way between bodies up the steps and out into the cool rain.

Soaked and shivering, he kicked the wall furiously. Galen needed him! He *had* to do something.

All at once the idea burst in his mind.

Soren must have sent it; she had made the trees, put seeds in the earth, sap in the veins. He breathed his thanks to her in relief.

Then he went back to the ivy.

He had to work a long time to wake it. It was sluggish, sleepy; it twisted away from him. It had forgotten the keepers, had been asleep too long, was too tired now ... Patiently, Raffi squatted by the gnarled stem, fingers in the cracks, telling it over and over what he wanted it to do, explaining every detail as if to a tiny child. It was young, he knew, and the power of the Makers was weak in it; it had no memory like the old yew-man that had once talked to him. But something was there. He argued with it, coaxed it, ordered it, went on repeating the task.

The leaves sighed, as if a breeze moved them. It moaned and complained and then, reluctantly, a tendril began to creep in through the broken window.

Breathless, willing it on, Raffi gripped the sill and watched it, the thin bine with its tiny glossy leaves slithering jerkily down the wall, along the floor, between benches, boots, table-legs, behind settles, dragging through the filthy straw. It stopped once, and the drowsiness of forgetting came to him, a great weariness and confusion, but he insisted and it moved again, rustling, tapping, ten years' growth in ten minutes, a mighty outpouring of its green effort.

Now it was under the Sekoi's chair, blocked by people passing from his sight. He moved, impatiently.

A corkscrew of leaves was climbing up the chair leg.

A roar of laughter burst out somewhere in the room. Raffi held his breath. The ivy curled, slithering up, out into the air, feeling its way. Delicately it wrapped a frail bracelet round the Sekoi's wrist.

For an instant, the creature went rigid. Then it picked up a card, put another down and dropped its hand below the table. It glanced round swiftly, then to the left, then across the room till its eyes came to the window and met Raffi's. He made a quick slash with his finger across his throat and jabbed it towards the Sekoi's back.

With a wry smile the creature looked down.

Raffi ducked under the sill, cold with relief. The creature's sharp, striped face had made not a flicker of surprise – no wonder it won at cards, he thought happily. But the fur on its neck seemed thicker, even from here. He prayed Godric hadn't seen him.

Already the ivy was falling back into sleep. He thanked it gravely and peeped in at the window again. The Sekoi said something to the player on its left, put down its cards and spread them with a wicked grin. The groan of the others was loud enough to hear outside. As it gathered the money, it stood and flashed one look into a mirror on the wall, instant and sharp. But that was enough. It would have seen Godric.

Raffi crept away. He was soaked to the skin and tired; the ivy had been harder to wake than he'd thought. And it wasn't over. When the Sekoi came out, Alberic's man would follow. He needed to think of something else now. The man was armed, after all.

Wearily, he crouched by the door and tried to plan, seeing all at once how late it was, how the sun had nearly gone. Moths danced in the smoky entrance; above the dim roofs flittermice squeaked and flapped. Galen would be getting worried.

After a few minutes he realized, stupidly, that no one had come out – and that all the noise in the room had stopped. Only the bang and clatter of the closing market came to him.

Suddenly afraid, he went to the steps and peered in. The room was dim. Fires crackled. Pipe smoke hung in thick blue layers. The Sekoi was sitting on the card-table, its long knees bent up over a chair. It was telling a story.

Everyone in the room was silent, listening intently. Only the jugs of ale moved, up and down as the men drank, absorbed in watching the creature's strange, spread hands, its keen yellow gaze. It spoke quietly, but with an odd hypnotic purr in its voice, and as he came down close enough to hear it, some vague anxiety drifted out of Raffi's memory like smoke, and all that remained was the story.

It was dark, and he was in a forest that spread endlessly all round him, and he knew his left arm was torn and bleeding. Far down between the trees evil things moved; they were creeping closer, the horrors that Kest had bred, things that slid and slithered and lurched through the wood. His skin prickled; he scratched his face and it was furred. A great sword hung heavy from his seven-fingered hand.

Out of the forest came a screech so savage it made him shiver. He lifted the sword and waited, seeing the starlight gleam on the cold metal, the fur on his neck prickling, and he snarled, his eyes watching the approaching shapes that crackled through the undergrowth. The darkness was thick, poisoned with steams and smoke; he strained to see through it, every crisp leaf breaking, a glimpse of slithering tail, scaled claw.

Then, out of the leaves the thing rose. A wyvern of Kest, huge, its wide wings blotting out the moons, the cold triplet of its eyes high above him, its scaly neck oozing blood and pus from the wounds the Cat-lords had dealt it. They were dead, his own sweet princes, and it still lived, and his anger at that was so raw that he raised the sword with both hands and swung it at the beast, screaming, but it put out a great claw and caught his shoulder and said, 'Raffi. Raffi! For Flains' sake boy, listen to me!'

53

Gasping, tears running down his face, Raffi stared at the Sekoi.

It grinned, smugly. 'You're back.'

Slowly, bewildered, he lowered his empty hands. 'What was . . . who . . . ?'

'You call him Kalimar. Last survivor of the Battle of the Ringrock. You know the story.' It glanced round darkly. 'Come on now, before they stir.'

Gripping his sleeve with its long fingers it hurried him away from the inn – he realized suddenly they were outside – and between the houses. The market was gone; the muddy ground trampled with straw and scraps of vegetables.

Raffi shook his head. 'The story didn't finish . . .'

'Didn't have to. They all knew it. Start them off and leave them to it, small keeper.' It looked pleased with itself; walked with a strange satisfied swing through the shadows, the fat purse bulging an inside pocket. 'Could have been sticky though. So Alberic's looking for us, is he?'

Raffi nodded. He still felt stunned; waves of anger and grief flooded him and he felt sick. The Sekoi glanced down, curiously. 'You were far in, small keeper. Too far.'

'I hadn't meant to listen.'

The Sekoi grinned. 'They all say that. Where's Galen?'

'Galen!' Raffi stumbled. 'He's sick. A Kest-claw bit him on the hand.'

The creature made a spitting noise in its throat. 'Ack! Then we should hurry. He'll need keeping warm. Is he delirious?'

'No. He's had it before.'

'Maybe, but it's always serious, Raffi. We should –'

It stopped, abruptly. Then it turned its head.

54

A man was standing in the gloomy lane behind them, dim against the trees. A burly man in a dark coat. He held a loaded crossbow, and it was pointing straight at Raffi.

'I didn't mean to listen either,' he said gruffly. 'I've heard your stories before, Master Greycat. It was hard, but my hood was up and one ear pressed against the settle drowned out most of it.'

The Sekoi hissed a spit of annoyance. It glanced round quickly. The village was silent. No one was about.

'Now what?' Raffi muttered.

'No spells, boy. No keeper-tricks or this bolt flies. I won't kill you, but Alberic won't mind damaged goods.' He leered. 'He's got plans to do a little damage of his own. Now, against that wall.'

The Sekoi backed, and Raffi followed. He still felt dizzy, and glimpses of the story kept flashing back at him – the wyvern, the forest, the sudden weight of the sword – as if this was all part of it, or he was in two places at once.

Then the field-wall was hard against his back.

Godric stepped closer. 'Where's the other one?'

Neither of them told him. He shrugged. 'We'll get him. Alberic has patrols out; the little man's spitting venom for you three, and the magic box of tricks.' But his eye was on the Sekoi, and Raffi knew all at once something else was on his mind.

'Tell me where he is, or I tie you up and we move out now.' But the man didn't move, and he was looking at the gold. Raffi felt a sudden quiver of hope.

Godric edged forward. 'Won a lot, didn't you?'

The Sekoi's fur rose silently round its neck. 'I was lucky,' it muttered.

'So I saw.' Suddenly he lowered the bolt, just a fraction. 'All right. Listen. Give me the gold, and you and the boy go free. I never even set eyes on you. Agreed?'

The Sekoi gave an eerie low hiss – a terrifying sound.

'Never,' it breathed.

'I mean it.'

'So do I.' The creature's eyes were slits, dark as chasms.

Raffi's heart sank.

'Suit yourself. I'll take it anyway.'

But like lightning the Sekoi moved; it turned and was gone instantly into the dark. With an oath of fury Godric leapt in and grabbed Raffi; a great arm tugged his hair back, the crossbow bolt pressed horrifyingly into his back.

Raffi froze; only the slightest of pressures would have set it off.

'The gold!' Godric roared. 'Put it down in the road or I kill him!'

There was a long silence. Then the Sekoi's voice came, strangled and odd from somewhere close. 'I'm sorry, Raffi,' it said.

'You can't just leave me!' he yelled, appalled.

He could almost feel the Sekoi squirm. 'The gold,' it hissed. 'I have to keep the gold!'

'You scum.' Godric spat in disgust. 'What do you people do with it all? Alberic would love to find the Hidden Hoard. Does it exist, Greycat? Is it real?'

'Alberic could drown in it,' the creature purred.

'Could he!' Godric sounded tight with anger. The crossbow quivered; Raffi gripped his hands together.

But the bolt that shattered the darkness was

blue; an enormous flash that burst in his head like a flame, and as blackness crashed back he felt the wyvern again, roaring and falling down upon him, into some endless pit.

7

Let the keeper own nothing but his faith.
For the Sekoi hoard gold
and men desire goods,
but the dew on the early grass
is a treasure beyond price.

Litany of the Makers

When Raffi woke up he found himself wrapped in
his own coat on a damp bank of dead leaves; they
rustled and crisped as he uncurled. Above him,
smooth trunks of beech trees rose into darkness,
stars glinting through their tangled branches.

For a moment he lay still, staring up; then a
crackle of sticks made fear break out of him like
sweat. He rolled over.

Galen was sitting by a small bright fire. He was
shivering as if he couldn't stop, huddled over some
cup of steaming drink, but when he looked across
there was the flicker of a grin on his face.

'So you're back with us, are you?'

Raffi propped himself up. He felt strange. One
side of his head and one shoulder were numb. His
left hand tingled.

'Did you fire the blue box?' he asked, slowly.

Galen nodded. 'Nothing else I could do. But he
was holding you too close – you caught some of
the blast.' He laughed grimly, and spat into the
flames. 'A good thing dear Alberic didn't use it all
up.'

'Did it kill him?'

Galen threw him an irritated glance. 'I'm not the Watch, boy. He's over there.'

Turning, Raffi realised that the fire was burning in a hollow among beech trees. Propped against one, well tied at the ankles, was Godric. The big man's head lolled to one side, and a few dead leaves had fallen on his hair and chest. But he breathed evenly.

Next to him, picking elegantly at a plate of berries, was the Sekoi.

'You!' Raffi jerked upright, suddenly furious. 'What were you doing! You would have let him kill me!'

The Sekoi spat out a pip. 'Nonsense,' it muttered.

'Did you see what happened?' Raffi turned on Galen.

'No. What?' he said quietly.

'Godric offered to let me go if that ... creature gave him the gold. A great bag of it. And it wouldn't! It just said "Sorry, Raffi"!'

Even now, he could barely believe it.

Galen was silent.

The Sekoi wrinkled its nose and waved a hand. 'Small keeper, work it out! What if I had given him my gold? Do you really think he'd have trotted back to Alberic saying "I haven't seen them"? Nonsense. We'd have lost you and it.'

'Well you wouldn't have cared about me!'

'Raffi ...' Galen growled.

'He wouldn't! It was the gold, that was all that mattered! I knew! I could feel it!'

The Sekoi glowered, its fur puffed out, but it folded its long arms calmly across its chest. 'Oh you could, could you?'

'Yes.'

'Clever. Not many keepers can read the Sekoi.'

Galen scowled. 'That's enough.' He tipped the dregs of his drink angrily into the flames. 'I don't know what went on. I only know Raffi feels betrayed and you . . .' he glanced at the creature darkly, 'you feel some sort of regret.'

The Sekoi shrugged. 'I have nothing to regret.'

'Thanks to me. However, the boy is right. We need to know where we stand. In my experience, the Sekoi have always hated the Watch.'

'They enslaved us,' it spat.

'They did. But the Order . . .'

It waved a hand, irritably. 'We have no quarrel with the Order, Galen. We are friends, you and I. And the small one. I would not betray you.'

'Nevertheless,' Galen pushed the damp hair restlessly from his face. 'I know the Sekoi. About gold, you can never be trusted. Your loyalty to that goes beyond any friendship with us. I understand that. The boy is too young to know yet.'

The Sekoi squirmed. Finally it said, 'It may be. Some things are too sacred to speak about.' It looked up, its yellow eyes sharp in the flamelight. 'I'm sorry, Raffi, Galen is right. I am your friend and always will be, but we have our own beliefs and gold is . . . vital to them. I can't explain why. Galen says we cannot be trusted. I would say, regretfully, that may be, but we are all of us on the same side.'

'And if the Watch offered you enough gold to give us up?' Raffi snapped, rubbing his arms savagely. 'What then? You'd do it, would you?'

The Sekoi was silent. It scratched its tattooed fur thoughtfully. At last it said, 'Let me put it this way. If I was in trouble, you would help me, yes?'

'Of course I would! I'd never – '

'Yes. Yes. But if the price of rescuing me was to give up the secrets of the Order? All the hidden knowledge? To betray your master, all the

Makers? Would you do that, Raffi, just to save me?'

He felt foolish, confused. Glancing at Galen was no help. He ran his hands through his hair, dragging out leaves. 'I don't know,' he muttered at last.

'No, you don't. It would be a fearsome choice. Always, you would try for some other way out.' It leaned forward, towards the flames.

'You must understand that we Sekoi also have our secrets, our beliefs, and the purpose of the Great Hoard is one of them. It may only be a metal to you. To us it is more, much more. It is our deepest dream. And every one of us is sworn to add to it, coin by coin, ounce by shining ounce until . . .' It stopped and smiled. 'Well, I can say no more. But you understand? For a second, back there, when he asked me for the gold, I was on the edge of that fearsome choice.'

Raffi was silent.

The flames crackled, glowing against the smooth brown boles of the beeches. And quite suddenly, out of his confusion and annoyance, he saw Carys, walking up some endless stairway, round and round, carrying a torch of pitch that dripped and crackled. She looked at him sideways, and she was scared, her eyes alert. 'The Interrex!' she hissed. 'Keep your mind on the job, Raffi!'

And then all he was staring at was a beech tree.

'What was it?' Galen had hold of him already. 'What was that! That was Maker-sent.'

Raffi took a deep breath. The Sekoi watched them both with interest. 'Some vision?' it murmured.

'I saw Carys. Climbing a stair. She reminded me about the Interrex. That was all.'

Galen bowed his head. 'My fault. We should have been moving faster!'

'But you couldn't. And where, anyway?'

'At least I know that. The only way to find out where the child is is to make a pilgrimage to the well. Artelan's Well.'

He touched the black and green beads at his neck. 'I hear your rebuke, Flain.' Suddenly he looked exhausted. He leaned back against a tree and said, 'Tomorrow. We leave tomorrow.'

'You should sleep.' The Sekoi came and laid its long hand over his forehead, and then at his wrists. Galen shook it off, but it grinned. 'My cure is working. You're less hot.'

'I wish I were even a little hot, Greycat.'

The growl came from the darkness; turning, they saw Godric was awake and watching them. The Sekoi snarled, 'That's not my name.'

But it threw Godric his cloak, a firm bundle that he had to catch hastily. Unruffled, he shook it out and wrapped it around himself. 'Much better. And something to eat?' He rubbed one hand over his beard, watching Galen closely. 'You owe me that, keeper, after nearly killing me with your relic.'

Galen gave a weary nod.

Raffi took the last of the berries over and dumped them down.

Godric gazed down in disgust. 'Flainsteeth! Is this all you people eat? Alberic's dog gets more than this!' He looked up. 'You should have let me take you prisoner, lad.'

Raffi tried to look uncaring. 'Keepers have higher things to think of than food.'

'Ha!' The big man roared noisily. 'By God, Galen Harn, your boy's either well-beaten or an idiot. Pass me that satchel, Greycat. It looks like I'll have to start feeding my captors. It's a new one, I'll admit – Alberic will love it.'

With a scowl at Galen, the Sekoi rummaged

through the pack for weapons, then hurled it over. Godric pulled out some fruit and small packages. They were wrapped in fresh calarna leaves and smelled superb.

'Venison. Smoked and stuffed. From the market.' He filled his mouth and pushed a package at Raffi. 'Go on, boy, eat some. You're just skin and bone.'

Raffi shook his head, doggedly, but Galen's voice muttered, 'Do as he says.'

Astonished, Raffi looked round. Galen was still leaning against the tree. His shivering seemed to have stopped, but he looked gaunt and weary. 'Go on. Eat.'

Godric wiped grease from his beard with the back of one hand. 'You too. And you, Cat.'

'We don't eat meat,' the Sekoi said haughtily.

'I'd heard that.' The big man hauled out a wine flask and drank noisily. 'Afraid you'd like it too much, eh?'

Raffi was barely listening. The meat was delicious, rich and tender and sweetened with herbs and salt; he swallowed every mouthful slowly, savouring the taste, licking every scrap off his fingers.

Godric watched him in real wonder. 'Here,' he growled, 'have more.' He glanced over at Galen and said grimly, 'I'll tell you this, keeper, we may be thieves but we take more care of our own than you do.'

Galen watched, his dark eyes level and unmoved. All he said was, 'We move on tomorrow. We'll leave you tied here, your weapons in that bush. You're near the road. You can shout. Eventually someone will hear you.'

'Probably the Watch!'

Galen nodded, gravely. 'Your problem. Tell

Alberic that he won't find us and that he will never get the box back.'

Godric snorted. 'It's you he wants!'

'Tell him. And next time he won't find his men left for him.'

'Next time he'll come himself.' Godric drank heavily, and stretched out his legs. 'You've made a bad enemy in the dwarf, keeper. Alberic has a puny body but big ideas. He rules because everyone's afraid of him. He'll ride out here with the whole thief-band when he knows you're here. And he won't go back without you.' He laughed, loudly. 'In pieces, probably.'

'We're used to being hunted.' Galen rolled over, wrapping the coat around him. 'Will you watch?' he said to the Sekoi, sounding bone weary.

'I'll watch. Go to sleep.'

As Raffi swallowed the last scrap of meat, Godric leaned towards him, clutching the flask. 'Do yourself a favour, lad,' he whispered, his breath stinking of ale. 'Leave this lot. Both of them care more about their dreams than about you.' He clapped a great hand on Raffi's hair and ruffled it. 'Clear out with me. Be a thief. If you like to live well, that's the life, boy.' Drunkenly he leaned back, closing his eyes. 'After all, what have you got to lose? You're an outlaw already.'

Jerking back, Raffi glared down at him bitterly. 'Thanks,' he said. 'Thanks a lot.'

The Tower of Song

8

*For Flain, the city of Tasceron, gold and
sunlit;
For Tamar, Isel's mountain, cold and high.
For Soren, the Pavilion of Song in the
green hills;
For Theriss, the blue chasms of the sea.
For Kest, the plain of Maar, abode of
horrors.
Above them all the seven moons,
and the Crow, flying between.*

Litany of the Makers

It had been raining all day, and there was no sign
of it stopping. Carys had given up; her hood hung
useless and her hair streamed, trickling and dripping inside her soaked clothes. Shivering, she
urged her horse on, seeing how the water oozed
and bubbled out of the leather of her gloves.

Ahead, under a stand of black-leaved saltan
trees, Braylwin and his three men were waiting.
Wearily her horse splashed up to them, and she
saw how the beasts' red paint had smeared and
dripped into the puddles below.

'Problem?' Braylwin asked absently. He was
dressed in a vast black travelling cape that hung
down below his stirrups; the rain pattered off it in
torrents. It was stiff with wax.

'He's going lame.' She slipped off, knee-deep in
water.

Braylwin shook his head. 'I've told you before

to get yourself a better horse,' he said crisply, above the downpour. 'And clothes, Carys! I like my patrol to be well turned out.'

Crouched over the horse's hoof, she snapped, 'I'm not as rich as you.'

'Ah, but that's your fault, sweetie. Prize money is only the half of it. The small gifts of the people, the bribes, the little inducements. Your trouble, Carys, is being too long among keepers.'

She dropped the hoof and slapped the horse's flank, then glared up. 'That's my business.'

His round face smiled down at her. 'Is it?'

'How far are we from this wretched place!' she asked sullenly.

'How far?' He took a plump hand off the reins and pointed. 'We're here.'

She stared out. Indistinct in the rain, grey in the misty drizzle, she saw a vastness, a great rising shape. At first she had thought it was cloud, a great bank of fog drifting up over the mountains, but now she realized with a cold awe that it was real, a vast building climbing the mountainside, rising in a countless series of rooms, stairways, balconies and galleries, far away and immense, its topmost roofs white with snow. And up there, like a needle sharp with ice, one uttermost pinnacle flew the remote black pennant of the Watch.

The Tower of Song.

How Galen would have loved this, she thought, the rain running into her eyes and down her face, the heavy downpour hissing from the low grey skies. How it would have amazed Raffi. They'd have prayed, she thought wryly. Looking up at the vast, rain-clouded walls of it, she almost wanted to pray as well.

Braylwin had been watching her. Now, as the rain began to crash with a new ferocity, he turned his horse hastily. 'Come on,' he called irritably. 'Before we drown out here.'

She walked, leading her horse up the steep mountain track. The tower loomed above; she saw how it had been built over centuries, been added to, repaired, ruined, neglected, renovated. All the Emperors had spent their summers here, far from the heats of Tasceron, building their palace of luxuries around the lost core of Soren's pavilion, the place she had chosen for her own when the Makers divided the Finished Lands between them, long ago. Now the Watch held it, one of their greatest fastnesses, and here were stored rooms of confiscated tribute, loot, treasures. And the records, the vast bureaucracy of files and papers and reports of its millions of agents. If she really wanted to find out about herself, about the Watch, about the Interrex, this would be the place. But she'd have to be careful. Very careful.

Hauling the horse up over the slippery pebbles, she wiped her face and scowled up at Braylwin's back. He came here every year for his winter quarters, warm and dry. Here they'd stay – until she had word from Galen. Irritated, she shook her head. She should have warned Galen.

It took an hour to clamber up to the outer barbican, and another half an hour to satisfy the searchers, fill in identity forms, get their papers and permissions and passes to the inner courtyards.

Trailing behind Braylwin across the cobbled yards and under the porticoes, she was amazed at the crowds of people: scribes, clerks, scriveners, translators. There were men dragging great trolley-loads of papers, long queues at doors, crowds round notices pinned to hundreds of boards. Most of them were sleek and well-fed; only a few were field-agents or post-riders, looking far more weatherworn. Climbing one vast staircase, she looked down and saw an endless miserable queue disappearing under one porch – not Watch, but tired-looking men, haggard women, a few lounging Sekoi.

'What are they?'

Braylwin paused long enough to glance down. 'Petitioners. People looking for their families. Criminals. No-hopers.'

He climbed on, clumsily. After a minute she ran after him.

His apartments were about a mile into the labyrinth of rooms and corridors they called the Underpalace; she realized after a while that even with all her training she was hopelessly lost. When they got there he went along a narrow passageway, banging doors open, tutting over dust, fussing at ornaments that weren't where he'd left them. She knew the men-at-arms would sleep outside his door when on duty, otherwise in the endless dormitories all Watchholds had. She was expecting that for herself, but Braylwin beckoned her coyly to the end of the corridor and flung a door open. 'For you, sweetie.'

She peered in.

A tiny room, with a bed and an empty hearth and a chest, and rain dripping into a pool, but when she'd crossed to the window and looked out she smiled, for the room was high in some turret, and it hung out into the sky over the tangle of lanes and courtyards and alleys far below.

She was glad it was up on its own. She was already beginning to dislike the Tower of Song.

'It'll do,' she said, turning.

Braylwin smirked from the door. 'Yes. For keeping an eye on you, Carys.'

It took her three days even to find a map of the

place. In the mornings Braylwin would dictate long reports of the summer's tax-gatherings to a harassed clerk who had been ordered to work with him.

The man deserved a medal, Carys thought darkly, watching the sleek Watchleader tease and flatter and make a fool of him. Harnor, his name was. Once she saw him give her a quick, exasperated glance, but he never lost his temper, and Braylwin smirked and preened and invented endless imaginary accounts until he tired of the game and sent one of the men-at-arms to fetch his dinner. After that he spent the long wet afternoons sleeping, or entertaining the gaggle of unpleasant cronies he called friends.

Carys was rarely needed, but he kept her hanging around; only in the afternoons could she vanish without suspicion. 'Take a tootle round,' he said once, filing his broad nails. 'This place is a labyrinth, Carys, you'll never find anything you need in it. Your friend Galen will love it, when we bring him in.' And he winked at her, so that she wanted to spit.

One thing she realized soon was that the rain here was eternal. The weather must have changed since the Emperor's time, because now the Tower loomed constantly in its cloud of drizzle; all the long afternoons rain trickled in runnels and gutters and spouts, spattering through gargoyles of hideous beasts and goblins that spat far down on the heads of hurrying clerks. Always the roofs ran with water; it dripped and plopped and splashed through culverts and drains, or sheeted down, a relentless liquid gurgle that never stopped, until she started to imagine that this was the song the tower sang, through all the throats and mouths and pipes of its endless body.

At first she wandered without direction, just trying to find her way back to the nearest courtyard, but she soon realized that was hopeless; once it took her three hours to find Braylwin's rooms again.

As she climbed the stairs wearily, Harnor was coming out.

'How do you find your way round this warren?' she snapped.

He looked at her in surprise. 'The maps. How else?'

'Maps? Where?'

For a moment he glanced at her. Then he pushed the thick folder of paper under one arm. 'I'll show you.'

He led her down three stairways and along a gallery which had once been painted with brilliant birds. Now only the ghosts of them lingered and great damp patches of lichen were furring them over. At the end he stopped and opened a small door. 'There's one in here.'

She went in after him, warily, but through the door was nothing but a balcony, and looking down from it she saw she was above a great echoing hall, full of desks and the murmur of voices. Coins were being counted down there, millions of them. She grinned, thinking of the Sekoi.

'This is the map. There are many, and they're scattered around the Underpalace. Would you like some paper? You could make a copy. It takes a while to find your way round otherwise.'

As Harnor rifled through the file for a clean sheet, Carys watched him curiously. He looked pale, as if he never went outside. He found a piece and gave it to her.

'Thanks. How long have you been here, Watchman?'

'All my life.' He smiled, sourly. 'Forty years and more. Once I hoped I'd be a field agent, but not any more. Too old.'

She nodded, looking up at the map: an immense sprawl of rooms and courtyards painted on the wall, each with its name in silver. 'This isn't Watchwork.'

'It's from the Emperor's time. There are many remnants of those days scattered round. Most have been destroyed but the place is so huge . . .'

'Have you ever explored it all?' she asked quietly.

He looked up, a strange, almost frightened look. 'Of course not. No one has. There are places that are not allowed.'

Carys had turned and begun to draw; now her pencil stopped. 'What places?'

He looked uneasy. 'The Great Library . . . and others. I'm not sure, really.'

She looked at him. He was small, his hair greying early, his beard clipped. He looked away. 'Is that all?'

She nodded, thoughtful. 'Thank you. Yes, that's all.'

Watching him hurry out, she knew he was afraid of her. That was normal. Everyone in the Watch spied on everyone else; it was their strength. But there had been something else; she had felt it instantly, that sliver of danger. She'd always been good at that. 'Top of the class again,' old Jellie had wheezed, back in the cold hall of the Watchhouse on Marn Mountain, and all the others in the class would stare, spiteful and envious and friendly, all the ones who had lived with her there, all the children the Watch had stolen . . .

She bit her lip, and went grimly back to the map. It took her an hour or so to make a copy, and even then it was rough and hasty. The names of the rooms enchanted her: the Gallery of Laughter – what was that like? And the Corridor of the Broken Vases – what had happened there? Even when she'd finished she knew this was only the Underpalace. There was far more than this: secret rooms and whole wings that needed extra passes even to get to. And above that the Overpalace, totally unknown. But it was a start.

Back in her room that night, chewing dainty filled rolls left from Braylwin's latest party, she lay on the bed and pored over the map, ignoring the relentless rain plopping into the filling bucket. Then she leaned back and gazed up at the ceiling. Where to begin? First she needed to find out about herself. And then – she frowned, because this was treachery, and if they knew it she'd be in deep trouble – then she had to find out if Galen was right. He said the Watch was evil.

And what did they do with all the relics they found? Destroyed them as abominations, she had always been taught; but since then, not only from Galen, she'd heard other things. That the relics were stored here, great rooms of them. That they held real power. She scowled, knowing she'd seen that for herself. And another rumour, never spoken out loud, only hinted at. That the Watch had a Ruler; that somewhere, above all the sergeants and castellans and committees and commanders and Watchlords there was someone else, someone secret, who knew everything. She shook her head. She'd never told this to Galen or Raffi, and even now she doubted it was true. But she had to find out.

Rolling over, she put a finger on the map, on a small corridor that ran north. That was the way. Higher up, there would be fewer people. She had a high clearance, she could certainly get that far. The corridor led to a place called the Hall of Moons. Under that, in Watch letters, was the word 'Births'. Tomorrow, she'd try there.

It was as she sat up and reached for another roll that she saw the eye. It stared at her out of the wall, unblinking, and for a second an ice-cold fear stabbed her, and she half-grabbed the bow, and then breathed out, and laughed at herself.

The eye watched her, clear and sharp.

Carys got up, and crossed to it. Taking a small knife from her pocket she reached up and hacked at the plaster; it was damp and fell in lumps.

Slowly the figure appeared, gorgeously painted in golds and reds; a great bearded man, carrying a black night-cub that struggled in his arms. She knew who he was. Tamar, the Maker who had made the animals. The one who had been the enemy of Kest.

She lay back on the bed and gazed at him. Two months ago, in Tasceron, Galen had spoken to these Makers. She had heard them answer him.

Or thought she had.

Long into the wet night, she stared at the figure on her wall.

9

In the form of an eagle he flew over Maar,
and saw how a great pit had been dug,
its maw smoking, full of strange cries.
Then Tamar felt fear, and he knew this
was in defiance of the Makers.

Book of the Seven Moons

'Going somewhere?'

Braylwin smiled at her sweetly over Harnor's shoulder.

She paused at the door. 'For a walk.'

'Ah, but where? Tell uncle.'

She scowled, but turned. 'I thought I'd do some intelligence gathering. About . . .' She glanced at the clerk's back. 'About that person Galen is looking for.'

'Ah!' She saw his face change. 'Good idea. Why not.'

But halfway out he called after her, 'I'll hear all about it when you get back.'

'I'm sure you will,' she muttered, and stalked down the corridor.

Five minutes later she knew he was having her followed. He wasn't using his own people, but a woman in a red dress – that was the one she was supposed to see – and a thin boy, the one she wasn't. She grinned. He was clever, but it was standard stuff. Maybe training was better these days.

She lost the woman in the Square of the Rainbow Fish, where there was a tatty scatter of stalls and food-sellers. The boy was more difficult. She knew she had to pretend she didn't know he was there, that he'd lost her by accident. She tried ducking through doorways and corridors, but he obviously knew the ways of the place more intimately than she did. Then she had a better idea. She'd let him follow.

Finding the Hall of Moons was bewildering, even with the map. She passed through endless halls, one so dark it was lit by candles, another piled with broken chairs, thousands of them, in some bizarre toppling structure, all interwoven, with a tunnel for passersby through the middle. The Passage of Nightmare, which she'd looked forward to seeing, was painted entirely black, and had no lights in it from one end to the other. She unslung her crossbow as she padded through it, and only three people passed her there, as if it was avoided. The Gallery of Tears ran with rain, dripping from the vast golden roof, so that the name still seemed right. She turned and climbed through whole labyrinths of corridors, always upwards, and once or twice when she passed through a wide square or long room she glimpsed the boy far back, clever, never obvious.

The Hall of Moons was barred by two great doors and two guards, the first she'd seen. A few people went in before her; her papers and insignia were scarcely glanced at. Being a Watchspy has its moments, Galen, she thought wryly.

Inside she stood still, utterly astonished.

The Hall of Moons was enormous, so vast the other end was barely visible in the gloomy light. Great windows reached from floor to ceiling on one side; on the other the wall was painted with seven gigantic images of the moons, the features of their surfaces, craters, humps, hills and valleys.

And holding these, as if they were toys, were the seven sisters themselves; Atelgar, Pyra, Lar, all of them, painted ten times lifesize in gold and cream.

Cautiously, she moved to a desk in the corner. A tall man looked down at her. 'Yes?'

'I want to see the records for a Watchhouse. Marn Mountain. 547.'

'Your clearance?'

She gave him the insignia, pulling the silver chain over her head. He glanced up, surprised. 'Your own house?'

'Yes.'

'This isn't usually allowed.'

'Even for the silver rank?'

He handed it back slowly. 'For what reason?'

Carys looked up at him. All at once she was angry. 'The reason is secret. If you're not able to help me, perhaps I should speak to your Watchmaster.'

The man almost winced. 'No need. I'll see to it,' he said quietly. 'Please take desk 246. I'll bring the record.'

She turned and stalked away, keeping her head up. When she found the desk she lounged there, looking round moodily. Maybe he'd report it. Maybe not. She didn't really care.

When the records came, they were in three enormous red books. She signed her name for them, then leafed through eagerly, but was soon disappointed.

Each year had the name of the children brought in, and their age, but that was all. No villages, no family names. All the children in Marn Mountain that year had the same surname – Arrin. It had been the castellan's name, that was why. Briefly she wondered about Carys, but there was no way of finding out.

When she found her own name and number she stared at them coldly for a long moment, as if they belonged to someone else. And in a way they did. It surprised her how bitter she felt then; the Watch had taken everything, her family, even her name. But the Rule said, 'The Watch is your name and your family.'

She slammed the book shut and tapped her fingers on it thoughtfully. She'd been stupid to think she could find anything here. They covered their tracks too well; they didn't want anyone to know too much. As for the Interrex, that would be hopeless.

Abruptly she got up, walked down the endless hall, passed the clerk without a glance and went out, into the labyrinth.

Braylwin was not impressed. Smoothing the sleeves of a new coat he watched her closely in the mirror. 'The Hall of Moons? I went there myself once, years ago. Were you looking for the Interrex, sweetie? Or something else?' His eyes were sharp in the plump face. 'Has little Carys been looking for her mummy?'

She ignored him. Instead she said, 'Have you ever been to the Overpalace? To the library?'

He shrugged. 'Never. It's not an easy place to get to. And there are no maps of the Overpalace – the place is almost unknowable. The Higher Watchlords may go there, maybe.' He grinned at her. 'All those delicious secrets, Carys.'

She nodded, thinking. 'It's guarded, of course.'

'Three bastions, each with a metal door. Once you get inside . . .' He turned, interested. 'Do you know what I was once told? Deep under the whole of this mountain are tunnels, a great network of them. Kest-creatures lurk down there, and some of them find their way up through to the passageways and corridors of the Overpalace. They're allowed to. They crawl about at night. Eat the odd spy, I suppose, or any fanatical keepers who get that far.' He was smirking, enjoying himself.

Suddenly she stared back at him, dubious. 'Stories to scare children, Braylwin.'

'Ah, but are they? Who knows what goes on in the Tower of Song – isn't that a proverb?' He turned back to the mirror and adjusted his sleeves. 'Even we in the Watch, beloved, don't know the half of this place. When it was first taken, patrols often got lost. One group starved; their bones were found days later. Bones, mind. Something ate them. And then there's the legend of the Lost Hall . . .'

'Go on,' she said drily, peeling a slim-fruit with her knife. She knew he was teasing her, that it might all be lies.

He examined a spot on his chin. 'It's a famous story round the tower. A captain called Feymir was drunk one night, wandered off and got lost. Next morning he put in a report about a great hall he'd found, chock full of Maker-gadgets. When he tried to find it again he couldn't. No one ever has. Whatever he'd been drinking, it must have been good.'

Outside the open window the rain was crashing on a roof.

Braylwin fiddled with his skullcap and stood back. 'What do you think?'

'Charming,' she said, eating peel.

He picked a pair of gloves off the table and swished to the door. 'Don't wait up!'

When he'd gone she hurled the knife after him in disgust. It embedded itself in the wood, vibrating.

Then, head on hands, she stared grimly out into the rain. What was wrong with her? She'd never felt so useless – as if she was some rat in a maze, going round and round and getting nowhere. Calm down, she told herself furiously. Think! The Tower worked on everyone like this; already she'd seen how the people who tried to find out anything in it went away hopeless, baffled, dulled into despair.

But it wouldn't happen to her!

For the next two days she read files, pored over reports, waded through endless, useless paper. Next she tried to get into the Overpalace. The first set of guards turned her back, despite arguments and passes and bribes. As a last resort she explored restlessly, walking for hours deep into quarters she'd not seen, once into a district not even on the map, a deep warren of disused kitchens and sculleries, down so many stairs they were probably underground. It was dark and empty, and it was down there, at one turn in a corridor, that she stopped, listening, the crossbow in her hands.

A distant, eerie howl had risen out of the floor, from far beneath. Silent, absolutely still, she waited, and at last it came again, indefinably closer, but muffled, as if layers of stone – rooms, dungeons, cellars – were between her and it. Not human. She crouched down with her ear to the stone slabs. Somewhere down there, unguessable levels below, something prowled. Tucking her hair back, she cradled the bow, her skin prickling with the menace of that wail. Whatever it was sounded hungry, and ferocious. After a while she stood up and walked on, the bow racked and loaded. Maybe Braylwin had been telling the truth after all.

Once more she thought she heard a similar thing, very faintly under the Corridor of Combs, but no one else there spoke about it, or even seemed to notice, hurrying past her with their arms full of papers.

Finally, she went back to her room late on the third afternoon, in despair, but Braylwin's snoring and the overflowing bucket in her room were too much. Furious, she flung the water out of the window and spun round, glaring at Tamor's bright eyes.

'What are you staring at?' she hissed. 'Can't you do something! Galen would say you could. Well, do it!'

Storming out, she leaned over a balcony in the Room of the Blue Rose and kicked the ornate balustrade. Crowds milled around her. No one spoke. In all this filthy anthill, no one cared about her – no one even knew her. Even Braylwin had given up having her followed. She wished, suddenly and fiercely, that Raffi was there, so she could talk to him, laugh with him. She'd forgotten the last time she'd laughed.

Then, just below her, she saw the clerk, Harnor. He crossed the room quickly, a file under one arm, and she called him, but he didn't hear. Suddenly she wanted to talk to him, to talk to anybody. She darted down the steps in time to see him vanish through a doorway, and she ran after him, pushing through the crowd.

Harnor was in a hurry. He was walking quickly, and she couldn't catch him until he'd crossed the Walk of the Graves and two courtyards.

By then she knew he didn't want to be seen.

He was going somewhere, and he was uneasy. He looked round too often and, passing the guard-posts, he seemed scared and alert. Carys kept back, interested. She began to trail him, using all the cunning of her training.

He went down a long corridor and through the

third door. Opening it gently, she saw this was some kind of store area – great cupboards and shelves overflowing with unsorted papers. There was no one in here. At the end of the room was a smaller door; through that she found steps, leading down into a damp passageway with a dead rat in the middle of it. Water dripped somewhere near.

Ahead, in the dimness, Harnor's thin shape padded.

She was intrigued. What was down here? And why was he so nervous about it? Twice she had to wait, breathless, as he stopped and stared back. At the end of the stone passage was a turning, then another. He walked quickly; he knew the way well. And then, as she peered round the last corner, she stared into dimness, astonished. It was a dead end.

But Harnor had vanished.

Carefully, Carys walked down after him.

The corridor ended abruptly; a stone wall with rainwater running down it in green seams. It was solid and firm, and so were the walls on each side; she ran her fingers along the greasy stones in amazement.

So where had he gone?

Suddenly she knew with a shiver of joy that this was important, this was what she had been searching for. Feverishly she pushed and prodded each stone, knelt and ran her hands round the joints and edges of the wall. And she felt a draught.

It was slight, but cold. Putting her fingers to it, she touched a wide crack lost in the blackness of one corner and found a small raised circle, smooth and warm. She knew it was Maker-work; there had been panels like this in the House of Trees. She took a deep breath, and pressed it.

Silently, with a smoothness that amazed her, a

section of wall melted. A small doorway stood there, and beyond it a room was pale with light.

Carefully, she lifted the crossbow, and stepped inside.

10

Promotion must be earned. Be ruthless;
there are many who will be passed over.

Rule of the Watch

She was standing in a dim hall. Light filtered
through one window high up in a wall; the rest
seemed shuttered or blocked.

The hall was crammed full of objects, piled high,
and someone was moving down in the shadows
among them. She heard steps, creaks, the bang of
something closing.

Creeping nearer, carefully, she found she was
moving between huge towers of dusty boxes,
ledgers, astrolabes, collections of skulls, hanging
maps that brushed her face with soft, cobwebby
edges. Ahead was a patch of light, oddly unflick-
ering. Silently, Carys crouched behind a wooden
crate and peered cautiously round.

Harnor was sitting at a tall desk, in a pool of
light from a lamp – a Maker lamp, which lit his
grey head and hunched shoulders with amazing
clarity. He was reading a great volume of thick
pages that turned with small stiff crackles. There
was no other sound at all. The hurrying queues
and crowds of the Tower seemed an eternity away.

Carys looked round, noting everything. Galen
might know what some of these things were – she
had no idea. There were boxes, panels, piles of
broken wiring, bizarre devices with screens and
buttons and dials which she knew were relics,
ancient things collected by the Emperors. There

were priceless books, marble statues, charts of trees and the complete skeleton of some small, unknown animal, as well as a globe showing Anara's continents, even the Unfinished ones, strange pieces of paper pinned all over it.

Harnor turned another page.

In the silence Carys scratched her cheek thoughtfully. Then she stood up and walked forwards into the light.

He was so engrossed that for a moment he didn't even notice her. When he did, his whole body jerked with terror; he leapt up, knocking the stool away with a smack that was deafening in the silence.

'You!' His eyes flickered over her shoulder, wide with fear. He seemed too choked to say anything clearly. 'How . . . did you . . .?'

'I followed you.' She perched on the edge of a table, the crossbow loose in her hands. 'You needn't worry. There's no one else with me.'

As soon as she'd said it, she realized she might have made a mistake. But he was terrified. He swallowed, rubbing his face feverishly, then took a step towards her. She raised the bow but he'd stopped already, gripping the desk as if to hold himself up.

'For God's sake,' he said hoarsely, 'for pity's sake, don't tell them!'

'I'm not surprised you're worried.'

'Don't play with me!' It broke from him like a cry of agony. 'I've got a wife, two children! What will happen to them! Think about them, please!'

'I'm not going to tell anyone.'

'But you're a spy. You work for Braylwin and if he . . .'

'If he knew, you'd be in chains so fast you wouldn't have time to blink, but I'm not him. I don't work for him.' She grinned. 'Haven't you noticed how he has me watched?'

Confused, Harnor clutched his head. 'Everyone is watched.'

'Except you, it seems. A small timid man nobody notices.' She waved the bow, curious. 'How long have you been coming here?'

He shrugged, then stammered 'I'm not sure . . . about twenty years.'

'Twenty years! Does anyone else know about it?'

'No.' For a moment his glance was proud, almost greedy. 'This is mine. No one else's. Except . . .' He put a hand to his head, hopelessly. 'Except you.'

Carys smiled. Deliberately she laid the bow on the floor and folded her arms. 'Listen to me, Harnor. I'm not investigating you. Finding this place was an accident. Sit down.'

He sat, numbly, as if he had suddenly become old, his hands clutched together, his thin face drawn. She could see the sweat on him. Leaning forward, she said quietly, 'Will you trust me?'

'What does it matter! You've found it all now.'

'I certainly have.' She glanced up at the towers of boxes. 'What is all this? Are they all relics? Are there other rooms?'

'Lots.' For a moment he stared down, bleakly. Then he began to speak and there was a faint edge of defiance in his voice, almost lost, but she caught it.

'I wanted to be a spy once. Out there, hunting outlaws, free, on my own. But they sent me here to keep accounts; year after year, petty records, endless reports, and I was weighed down by it, it buried me, closed over my head.' He stared hopelessly. 'You can't imagine that. You're too young. Oh, at first I was hopeful, I put in applications, I bribed people. I waited my life away, but it was all useless. I was too ordinary. Just a number, a small despairing pen-pusher no one cared about. I lost hope. This place does that to you.'

She nodded, swinging her foot. 'I'd noticed.'

'Well, think of spending decades here. All the years of your life.'

They were silent. Then he looked up. 'But somewhere, deep down, I wouldn't give in. I thought, if I'm trapped here, I'll make this place my adventure. I'll learn it, as no one else ever has. If there are secrets I'll find them.' He glanced at her, and she saw his eyes were very bright. 'I explored, Carys. I learned every corridor, every gallery. I spent years searching, all my spare time, planning, charting in my head, writing nothing down so they'd never know. And then, one day, I came into that corridor, and found the hidden door.'

He wasn't scared now. He was trembling, exultant. 'There are whole suites of rooms here no one knows about. All the things in them, the Emperors' things, the Maker-things, are mine. I've spent years with them, these statues. Look . . . look at this, how beautiful it is!'

He jumped up suddenly and, picking up a cube, thrust it into her hands. As she turned it she gasped, because trapped inside what seemed like glass was a whole landscape, a place of green fields and strange trees and the sky there was blue, a deep, perfect blue. It wasn't a flat picture. Somehow it was real.

'That's the home of the Makers, Carys, and there's more here, much more. It would take years to show you all of it; beautiful books, statues you almost think are watching you. I love these things. I've grown to love them.' He stopped abruptly and looked straight at her. 'I know it's wrong. But I do.'

She frowned, thinking how he had suddenly become alive, and then his eyes fell and he was Harnor again, aghast at seeing her there. To give herself time, she got up. 'Take me round,' she said.

For the next half hour each of them forgot all danger. Even Carys was dazzled by the treasures the rooms contained. Harnor had piled them all here, cleaned the frescoes and wall paintings so that they glowed: bright, colourful scenes of the world's Making that would have silenced Galen. There were wonderful fragments of sculpture, jewels, crystals, strange artifacts, bizarre machines, a whole collection of brilliant and intricate tapestries. Fingering a small device that clicked a flame on and off, she looked up and saw him watching her.

'Did you mean it?' he whispered. 'About not telling him?'

'I meant it.'

'Why?'

'Because I want you to help me.' She put the flame-maker in her pocket and sat herself in a huge, winged chair, feeling like some empress. 'You see, I'm a bit like you, Harnor. Not quite what I seem. You say you know the tower. I want you to get me to the Overpalace. To the Great Library.'

He stared at her in horror. 'But – '

'Do your passages go that far?'

Bewildered, he ran his hand down an exquisite silver figure. 'No . . . at least, well, yes they do. There are ways, but – '

'No buts. That's where we're going.'

'But why?'

'Because I want to find things out,' she said shortly. 'About who I am.'

To her surprise he laughed, a bitter laugh. 'Oh do you? Well you won't find anything.' Seeing her stare he looked away. 'You wouldn't be the first. Even I tried that. Many years ago. The library is dangerous to get into but I went there. Once was enough. There are no records, Carys. Each child's first name is entered and that's it. No one cares where they came from. It's not important.'

She got up, furious, and stalked over to a box and stood looking down, seeing nothing. What would you have done anyway? she asked herself coldly. Gone and found the village? Her parents? They wouldn't have even recognized her.

'We're still going,' she growled.

He glanced frantically round. 'You're crazy!'

'Listen, Harnor!' She turned on him, blazing with wrath. 'You're not the only one who breaks the rules. I know a keeper, well, two of them . . .'

He stared at her aghast. 'A keeper!'

'That's right. And he's made me think. Who is it that runs the Watch? What do they want with relics? Why stamp out the Order so savagely?'

He shrugged. 'Everyone knows the Order was evil.'

'But the relics! Think about it! They were once full of power, a power we know nothing about. The keepers do. I've seen that. What I want to know is why the Watch teaches us it doesn't exist!'

He shook his head in fear. 'I don't want to think about this.'

'Get me to the library, and you won't have to.' She came over, quickly. 'I'll go then. You'll never see me again. And you'll still have all your treasures.'

For a moment, seeing his despair, she felt like Braylwin and hated herself. But when he looked up his face was set.

'All right. But only once.' He looked bleakly at the silver fish under his hand. 'Be here tonight. And come armed.'

11

For a year they held me underground,
bound with chains.
They tried to enter my workrooms, but
the Pit was sealed.
My secrets lay deep. And they were well
guarded.

Sorrows of Kest

The rain was horizontal, crashing in sheets. Lightning flickered, white and silent. As Carys waited for the sleep-drug to take effect, she watched it from the window, hearing all the gutters and waterspouts of the tower gurgle their song. Far below, one dim torch burned in the corner of a courtyard.

The third time she checked, the man was asleep, propped on his bench outside Braylwin's door. She stepped over him, then went back and knocked the cup over with one foot, spilling the dregs. Just in case.

All the way she was careful; doubling back, going by narrow routes, quiet back alleys. No sign of anyone following. When she was sure, she went down into the stone corridors.

It took her a while to find the right dead-end, and when she slipped inside Harnor was waiting. He looked white and agitated.

'Where have you been!'

'Making sure I wasn't followed.' She settled the crossbow. 'Come on. I need to be back before morning.'

He fidgeted, anxious. 'Listen. There are things up there. Creatures. They roam the tunnels.'

'You said you'd been there before.'

'Years ago . . .'

'Well then, you can do it again.' She was sharp, irritated. 'Now come on!'

He gave her one miserable look and led the way to a door in the corner. She'd need to watch him, she thought. He could lead her anywhere down here. Try to lose her, even. 'Remember this, Harnor,' she muttered. 'You get me to the library, or I make sure Braylwin knows everything.'

For the first hour they barely spoke. He led her along filthy corridors and empty rooms, once across a courtyard choked with weeds, high wet walls all around them. Glancing up, she saw dark windows. All these empty rooms. The size of the place made her uneasy. Was it possible no one else knew about it?

They climbed stairs, vast wide steps and narrow spiral ones, lit by torches Harnor kept in various places. Halfway up one she stopped, so suddenly that Harnor stared back in terror. 'What? What is it?'

Carys stood still, not answering. For a moment she had seen something amazing, as if a panel had opened in her head. Raffi had been there, and Galen and the Sekoi, all around a fire under some dark trees, vivid and close. She could even smell the burned wood, and Raffi had turned and seen her and called something.

'Have you found the Interrex?' she whispered.

But he hadn't answered, and she couldn't see them now.

'What's the Interrex? Is it here?' Harnor stared round in agony.

'No.' She shook her head, absently. 'Forget it. Keep your mind on the job.'

As they climbed higher into the warren of rooms and galleries she thought about it, pacing through vast dim halls. Was that the third eye Raffi talked about? It was amazing. And what did it mean? Had they found the Interrex? Galen had said she would know, but was that it? So soon?

Then she realized Harnor had stopped. He was waiting by a gate, a grille of rusted metal. A small entrance had been made by twisting some of the bars. Beyond, the darkness was complete.

'Once in here,' he whispered, 'we're in the Over-palace. Or rather under it. About three floors below the inhabited parts. You should load your bow.' He took out an old curved knife from behind a stone. 'I'll have this.'

'So what's in there?' She racked the bow quickly.

He shivered, unhappy. 'Who knows. I've heard horrible noises, found droppings, chewed food, great holes torn in doors. Often I've thought I was watched.'

She nodded. 'But you've never seen anything?'

'Once I thought . . .' His hands shook on the knife. 'Each time, it was harder to come back. Last time I swore to myself I'd never come here again.'

'After this you won't have to.' She felt heartless, but she needed him. 'Right. Now lead on.'

It was darker here. Dust lay thick on the untrodden floors. Harnor seemed less sure of the way. Twice they doubled back through long galleries; once at a crossroads of four passages, he hesitated. Carys watched him gravely, and his eyes flickered to her in the dark.

And there were other things here. She knew it, with a growing instinct, all her training warning her. A scuttle in the dark, something that breathed

around a corner. They went slowly now, more carefully, and once were so near the inhabited rooms
she heard voices through a wall and muffled
laughter.

After about half an hour, she heard something
else. It was in the distance ahead of them, a regular
throbbing that echoed strangely in the passageways. 'What's that?' she murmured.

Harnor gave a wan smile. 'That won't hurt us.'

It grew louder as they walked, a cacophony of
knocks and ticks and chimes until, as he pulled
open a great door, the sound burst out and she
saw a vast hall full of clocks. There were thousands
of them, candle-clocks, sand-clocks, mechanical
clocks in every shape, all ticking at different rates,
different speeds, a bewilderment of noise.

Carys stared. 'Did you bring these all here?'

He shook his head, nervously. 'I found it like
this. I haven't been here for over a year. As I
said . . .'

She glanced at him in instant alarm. 'So who
winds them?'

He was aghast. He stared at her and went so
white she thought he would faint on the spot. 'I
didn't think of that,' he breathed.

'Fool!' Carys hissed. She couldn't help it. She
was furious with him. 'So much for your secrets!
How far to the library?'

'Ten minutes.' He was shaken, and wiped his
face with a damp hand. 'Should we turn back?' he
whispered. Then, 'Please, Carys.'

'No.'

They hurried through the Hall of Clocks. Shuffles moved in the darkness behind them. Harnor
was reckless with fear; Carys kept a sharper look-
out.

Halfway down one gallery he stopped.

95

'Here?' she whispered, surprised.

He raised the torch up and she saw a ladder: narrow metal rungs up the wall, climbing into darkness. 'Up there.'

She put the torch out, stamping it with her foot. After a second he did the same. The tunnel was dim with acrid smoke.

'You first,' she muttered.

He seemed to force his courage together; then he was climbing, a thin figure lost in the dimness. Carys put her foot on the lowest rung and her hands up. For a moment she looked sideways, into the dark.

Something slid. She could hear it, for a moment, a soft scaly sound. Then silence.

Hurriedly, she swarmed up after him.

The ladder was high: twenty, twenty-one rungs. Breathless, she clung tight and looked up. 'How far?'

Her hiss echoed as if they were in some great shaft or airwell.

'Nearly there.' He sounded as if he was struggling with some weight; a slot of paler dark opened above him, swung to a wedge, then crashed back to a great square and he climbed up through it and was gone.

Coming after him, she hoisted herself quickly through the hole and stood up, dusting her hands.

They were in the library.

It was vast; a series of enormous arched halls leading one out of the other, and down the centres of them great shelves rising to the roof, each crammed with books. After a moment she wandered along them, seeing thousands of volumes, each one held by a tiny chain, some lying open on the desks below. What secrets there must be here, she thought bitterly. And how could she look through them all? Where should she even start?

She turned on Harnor, a dim, nervous figure, the great windows behind him dripping with rain.

'Where are the most important books kept?' She came up close to him. 'Think! They're locked up, probably.'

He ran a hand through his grey hair, then turned reluctantly. 'Up here.'

Beneath the great ranks of books they felt small, uneasy. They walked quickly, conscious of the echoes of their footsteps, the endless patter of rain. Rats ran before them, scattering with tiny scuttering noises. Harnor hurried through three great halls; he came to a dais of three steps and stopped at the foot of it. 'Up there,' he gasped. 'But be quick, Carys. Be quick!'

She saw the seven circles of the moons on the wall, vast shapes of beaten copper, gold and bronze. Under them, standing in a long row, were the Makers. They looked down at her with huge dignified faces as she walked under them; and in the centre was Flain, his dark hair bound with silver, his coat shining with stars. In his hands he held a box, and coming up to it she saw there was a real door in the painting, a tiny door with a shining lock.

She grinned and fished in her pocket, took out a long thin wire and slid it into the keyhole.

'What are you doing!'

'Opening it. I always enjoyed those lessons.'

Harnor sank in a huddle on the steps; he seemed too terrified to speak.

The lock was difficult, but suddenly the wire clicked round and she laughed, pulling the door wide and putting her hands in.

Harnor squirmed round, fascinated. There were

piles of books in the safe, most of them rich with jewels and carved gems, too huge to lift, and she rummaged hurriedly among them, right to the bottom. She was still a moment; then she said, 'Look at this,' in such a strange voice that Harnor fought off his fear and scrambled up the steps, and he saw she held a relic in her hands, a very small, grey console with a blank screen. She brought it out carefully, knowing that this was precious, secret, something meant never to be seen. It had been burned once; its edges were black and scorched. Baffled, she turned it over.

'What is it?' Harnor muttered.

'I don't know. But Galen will.'

'Who's Galen?' he began, but then he stopped, staring over her shoulder, his face set in a sudden agony of terror.

She spun around.

Far down the halls, up through the open trap-door, something dark and long, endlessly long, was slithering.

12

*The creatures of the deep, how shall we
number them?
Beasts of nightmare, spun from the dark
mind.
All the spiny, envenomed things of anger.
They infest us, they breed.
Who will rid us of them now that the
Makers are gone?*

Poems of Anjar Kar

It rippled like a great worm, its fluid body thick
and loathsome. As they stared, the tail slid out of
the hole, whipping swiftly behind the dark book-
shelves.

Harnor looked ashen. 'God,' he kept muttering.
'Oh God.'

Carys stuffed the relic inside her coat and
grabbed him tight. 'Keep quiet. Quiet! And stay
close.'

He shuddered; she saw the knife blade quiver
in his hand. They stepped carefully down from
the dais, every nerve alert. She held the crossbow
ready.

Neither of them spoke.

On each side the vast black shelves loomed, the
creature winding invisibly among them. Faintly,
they could hear it; somewhere it was slithering, its
scales making a light, sinister hiss and scrape on
the stone floor. The sound seemed all around;
Carys, her fingers clutched on the bow trigger,
glanced nervously behind them.

Harnor jerked her arm in terror. 'There!'

She whirled, saw a length of something slide into shadow. Her fingers were wet with sweat; she knew if she fired and missed, it would be on them before she could reload. It was hunting them, whatever Kest-horror it was, rippling round them with its endless coils. Somewhere in the halls the narrow eyes would be watching, behind some tower of books, through some slit.

It stank, too: a sickening, putrid stench.

The black halls seemed enormous; far ahead in the darkness the trapdoor waited, a slanted square. It was their bait.

'We'll never make it,' he moaned.

'We're not meant to make it.' She was walking backwards now, the bolt spanning the shadows.

They came through the first hall, then the second. Small squirms and ripples of movement slid in the dark, out of sight. Carys's arms ached with tension.

Ahead, the doorway to the third hall loomed. They were almost under it when his choked yell made her leap round and instantly she saw it, towering over them: a great looping, uncoiling serpent, grotesque fins of small bones splaying from its neck, its great head flat like a snake's but crested with spines that dripped poisons and acids in pools on the floor, bubbling and hissing into the stone. Wide green eyes gleamed at her. She jerked back as the scorching saliva seared her face, then she aimed and shot the bolt straight at its throat.

Almost mocking, the head swerved aside; the bolt splintered something in the dark. Cursing, Carys scrabbled for another, but the worm darted straight at her, and with a gasp of terror she squirmed away, fell into a gap between shelves, picked herself up and ran.

Harnor was ahead, reckless in the dark. They raced the length of one passage, then swung into another before she hauled him down and they crouched, breathing hard, the darkness spitting and slithering all around them.

'Don't get lost!' She jammed the bolt in frantically. 'We have to get down that hole!'

'We can't.'

'We can! Don't panic. It's a beast – it has no reason.'

He was white; the knife trembled as he clutched it. She had to drag him to his feet but he crumpled again and cowered into the shadows, hands over his face. 'I can't. I can't. I'll stay here. I'll be all right.'

'It can smell you!' She hauled him up, furious. 'For Flain's sake, listen to me! Listen! We get through these shelves till we're opposite the trap. Understand? And don't get lost, Harnor, because I won't come looking for you.'

He stared at her in dread. Then he rubbed his face again. 'All right.'

They paced down rows of books. Halfway along one, Carys paused. The library was utterly silent, except for, far-off, the drumming of rain. Nothing moved. The silence was like an ache. And now she could smell the thing, a strong stench of rotting weed, stagnant water. Bending, she felt the stones of the floor. Her fingers touched a thick slime, an acrid smear that crossed before her and ran under the dark shelves.

Hurriedly she straightened and stepped over it. But the hall was criss-crossed with the worm's trail; soon the stench was on their hands and boots, a cold slime they couldn't rub off. By the time they crept to the crack in the shelves they were sick with it, Harnor retching with the back of one hand over his face. Sweating, she peered out.

Everything was still.

'Now,' she whispered. 'Stay together. We'll need both of us against this thing. Stab deep, but remember there are coils of it so don't stop. Just get down the ladder.'

He nodded, but she saw he was stupid with terror. Gripping the bow tight she said, 'Now. Run.'

He didn't move.

'Run!'

'It's out there. It's waiting.' His voice was a breath; he was staring out at the trapdoor like a man in a nightmare, frozen with panic. Suddenly she turned and shoved him, hard, out on to the dark floor so that he screeched and rolled and scrabbled in horror towards the square of darkness.

And instantly the creature was on him.

It swooped, out of some high place, and she was awed at the rippling speed of it, the glistening coils. Harnor shrieked; Carys fired the bolt hard, and it thumped into the creature's flesh but the thing didn't stop, it kept coming, and Carys pulled out her long knife and ran out, slashing at it. It hissed and spat; it was all around her, moving fast, bewildering, and suddenly she was entangled in it, the firm muscles slithering under her arms, around her knees. As she slashed, some coils loosened but others came, squeezing her tighter, slippery with slime and a cold watery blood.

'Harnor!' she screamed.

Then she saw him. He was halfway down the hole; for a second he looked up and saw her and she yelled at him again, and caught the furtive glimmer of his face, white as paper. Then he was gone, and she was being dragged, one arm trapped tight, kicking and fighting. She had no breath now; she squirmed and wriggled and then suddenly, instantly, lay limp.

The terrible squeezing slowed. Somewhere in the dark, a long hiss told her the head was zigzagging in.

Carefully, one-handed, she felt inside her pocket and pulled out the tiny firelighter she had picked up the night before. She felt choked; the cold grip of the contracting worm was suffocating all the anger out of her, but she waited until its head loomed above, spiralling down, the green eyes alight in the dark.

Then she flicked the lighter on.

The head whipped back.

She held it out, as far as her arm would reach; then, with a better idea, brought it back against the beast's skin. It convulsed into shivers, squeezing her harder, but she held the flame there, relentless, coughing at the burning of the scales and the acrid smoke, the tiny fierce Maker-light flaring blue and green. Then, with a jerk that almost broke her ribs, the creature opened up and flung her out, kinking and wriggling in irritation and she dived under it into the open square of the hole and fell, swinging with a scream and a crash against the ladder, grabbing again, the knife and bow clanging and clattering down into the darkness below.

Above her the creature searched frantically; as its body looped she hauled herself up and grabbed the trapdoor and with one great heave pulled it down over her, so that the blackness rang with the crash of falling dust.

For a long time she clung to the ladder, shaking, breathing hard. Above her the slither of scales

103

sounded faintly; she was sore and bruised, her legs weak with sickness and relief.

After a while, she felt calmer. Then she thought of Harnor. Where was he? She cursed him silently, calling him coward, craven little rat, and the anger put fresh strength into her; she found herself clambering down the slimy ladder, down the long descent into blackness until her feet met the stone floor abruptly.

She stood still.

'Harnor?'

The whisper echoed; she hadn't expected any answer. Moving cautiously, her foot nudged something. She bent and groped for it, her hands feeling it over. The crossbow. Dented. She took out the tiny fire-maker and flicked it on; the blue flame shone pale. After a longer search she found her knife and stuck it into her belt grimly. So he'd gone, then. And what a squirming panic he'd be in, running back through the silent rooms, sobbing with fear, dodging shadows, imagined slithers down the walls.

She smiled, remotely. Poor Harnor. Was this what the Watch had done to him, or had he always been afraid? Was that why they'd never trained him? How would she be without that training? She frowned. Anyway, he must think she was dead, or if not dead then lost, hopelessly lost in this labyrinth of rooms and tunnels and halls.

She grinned, pushing the grimy fringe from her eyes. Then she lit the torch propped against the wall and began to walk, the bow slung ready.

The first mark was on the corner of three passages; the torch light fell on it and she reached out and smudged it off, the chalk whitening her thumb. He hadn't seen them, then. She'd made them low, bending in snatched moments when he hadn't been looking, with the tiny lump of chalk she'd brought. If he'd been trained, he would have guessed.

'Always leave yourself a way out,' old Jellie would say, pounding up and down the icy classroom with his stick, crunching day-dreamers sharply in the back. 'Never rely on anyone else to get you out.'

She walked quickly, but the way seemed endless and she had no idea how much time had gone by. The rooms and halls were dark, and once or twice she had to search hard for the chalk-marks. Down in the dampest tunnels great slugs had crawled out; the torchlight flickered on them, white, flabby monsters. She ignored them, because they were no danger, but sometimes there were other sounds: a creak of wings in a high hall, muffled voices, and once a faint scuttling, as if some immense insect ran up an invisible wall.

The Hall of Clocks was a relief; she heard the tocking from far off and almost ran through the halls towards it, but when she'd squeezed through the twisted gate into the courtyard she was dismayed to see how light it was. Drizzle was falling, but it was well into the morning. Cursing, she kicked the weeds aside and raced for the opposite door, praying that Braylwin would still be asleep. In her hurry she took two wrong turns; it must have been over an hour before she came through the door into Harnor's cluttered secret halls. She dumped the worn-out torch into a corner and ran past the piled-up relics and smooth statues to the hidden sliding panel.

For a moment she thought he had locked it; then she realized she had never opened it from the inside, and it took her hasty, irritated minutes to find the catch.

Once out, she sped through the halls and courtyards. The tower was awake; a clock chimed ten, and she pushed through the crowds of clerks and waggonloads of files with rising despair.

Up the stairs, along the corridor, smoothing her hair, rubbing dirt from her face, and then as she turned the corner she saw Braylwin's door was open and heard his high plaintive voice whining inside.

'Well, where is she? How long has she been gone?'

Coming to the door, Carys peered in.

Braylwin was swelling with rage, his red silk gown bursting its buttons. The man-at-arms looked sour. In one corner Harnor was working, bent over his desk as if he wished he could disappear into it. He looked tired out, and terrified; he still wore the same clothes, and she could see the dried mud on his boots.

Braylwin took breath for another outburst. Then he saw her. 'There you are! Where on earth have you been?'

All heads turned.

Carys came in and looked at Harnor. She had never seen anyone cringe like this. For a moment their eyes met and she stared at him levelly, wanting him to feel the terror, the suspense. It was the only punishment she could give him; now she had to save herself, get herself out of the stifling tower before the loss of the relic was traced to her.

'Well?'

She perched on the table, and began picking at the remains of Braylwin's lavish breakfast. 'Out. I wanted to walk.'

Harnor almost collapsed in relief. Braylwin glared at him. 'You. Get on.' Looking back at Carys he said, 'So early?'

'Yes. I had to think.'

'About what?'

'About whether to tell you.' She looked up and gave him the best lie she could think of. 'I've had a message from Galen.'

Braylwin rubbed his fat hands. 'You have?'

'I have. We need to leave at once. He's found the Interrex.'

Artelan's Well

13

Always now, we will be hunted.
        Third Letter of Mardoc Archkeeper

Raffi waited anxiously by the door. The cottage was small; he could see the fire crackling inside, the dresser with its pewter plates, a basket of chopped wood. It looked cosy. For a moment it reminded him of home.

Then the woman came back, a toddler clutching her skirt. 'Here. Take these.' She dumped the rough sacking in his arms hastily. 'Cheese. Some smoked fish. Vegetables. That's all I can spare.'

'It's very generous,' Raffi muttered.

She gave him a hard looking-over, and he felt himself going red. 'Wait,' she said.

In a moment she was laying a blue jacket on the sack. 'That was my eldest's. It's too small for him now. You have it.'

He was really red by this time. 'Thanks,' he mumbled.

'You'd better hurry. My husband will be back and he won't stand for tramps. Which way are you heading?'

Off guard, he shrugged. 'West . . .'

The woman turned and gathered the child up on to her hip. 'Then be careful. The Watch are always patrolling that way.'

He nodded, walked to the gate and turned to say thanks again. She was looking after him, the baby playing with her hair. Suddenly he saw how young she was.

'Give us your blessing, keeper,' she whispered.

For an instant Raffi was still. Then he raised his hand, as he had seen Galen do, and said the Maker-words slowly, carefully. It made him feel strange. Older. She bowed her head, and without looking up, went back into the house.

Three fields away, under a blackthorn hedge, Galen looked sourly at the jacket.

'Keepers didn't use to have to beg for castoffs,' he said bitterly.

Raffi didn't care. He tried the jacket on. It was dark blue and warm, and even the patches were better than his old, worn coat, full of holes.

'She knew what you were?' the Sekoi asked quietly, nosing in the sack.

'She guessed. She said the Watch are about.'

Galen snorted. The burst of fever was over, but it hadn't improved his temper. He bit into a carrot. 'You said nothing else?'

'No.' But the memory of that word, 'West', stung him; Galen stopped chewing and stared harder. Then he leaned over and caught Raffi's arm. 'What else? What did you tell her?'

'Nothing . . .' But that was useless. He frowned and took a breath. 'That we were going west.'

For a moment he thought Galen would hit him. Then the keeper flung him away, his eyes black with fury.

'I didn't mean to! She caught me unaware!'

Galen gave a sour laugh. 'Never mind. Too late to start being careful now.'

'She won't tell anyone.'

'Let's hope not,' the Sekoi muttered, uneasily. It spat out the pips of a dewberry and stood up. 'Still, it would be best to be gone. How far is this magic well of yours?'

Galen flashed it a vicious glare. 'I don't know.'

'You've never been there?'

'No one's been there for years. It's lost.'

'Lost?'

'In the marshes.'

They both stared at him, but he flung the pack at Raffi and stalked off, his tall stick stabbing the mud.

The Sekoi gave a tiny mew of disgust. 'I should have taken my chances with Godric,' it muttered.

For two days they trudged through fields and scrawny pastures, always upwards. The weather was warm, and Raffi tied his new coat to the pack and watched the vast flocks of migrating mere-birds flying over, always west, their loud cries breaking the evening hush. But the nights were cold; once they lit a fire in a copse of oak trees that Galen said still had much Maker-life and were prepared to allow it.

By now they were high up, and the pasture was poor, full of hollows and humps, studded with boulders, cropped by hungry sheep. Four moons, wide apart, lit the sky.

For a change, Galen was in a milder mood. He was wrapped in his dark coat, the firelight making shadows move on his sharp, hooked face. The Sekoi asked its questions carefully, flipping a gold coin over in its fingers.

'So what is this lost well?'

The Relicmaster smiled, his long hair falling. 'It's a long story. Once there was a keeper; his name was Artelan. He had a vision and he saw Flain. Flain told him to travel far to the west, to the edge of the Finished Lands, and he would find an island called Sarres where fruit grew all year, where there was no snow, no strong winds, a place out of the world. And on the island was a well, and whoever drank out of it would have his questions answered.'

'So he went?'

'He went. The story of his adventures is a long one, but finally he climbed these hills and on the other side saw the Moors of Kadar, green and fertile. And rising out of them was a strange hill, remote and eerie, looking like an island in the mist, and Artelan travelled there, and they say he found the spring and the fruit trees, just as Flain had said. I've often found it odd, though, that Flain should say it was an island.'

The Sekoi smiled, scratching its zigzag tribemark with one finger. 'You people waste your stories. I could tell this so that we would all seem to be there now.'

Galen nodded. 'Our gifts are different. But the Makers gave them all.'

'They did not!' It sat up fiercely. 'Not ours!'

Galen frowned but Raffi said, 'Never mind all that. Tell us more about the well.'

This time they both glared at him, but he didn't mind. He was warm in his new coat and a blanket, and the soft crackle of the fire soothed him. Galen dragged his hair back irritably. 'It became a place of pilgrimage, a holy place. The Order built a great house there, and a custodian lived there always. People came, looking for peace, some of them for healing. When they came back they were different. The well had given them wisdom.'

'And you think it will tell us where this Interrex is?' The Sekoi looked politely dubious.

'Me. It will tell me.' He was silent for a moment, then shifted, so the green and black awen-beads glinted. 'If it still exists. Because the Watch have destroyed us, and who knows what happened there. Artelan once wrote that the spring would

114

never fail, and never be foul. Let's hope the Watch never found it.'

'What would have stopped them?' Raffi asked sleepily.

Galen gave him a strange look. But he didn't answer.

Raffi was silent too. He'd had a sudden mind-flicker; it was water, the shimmer of it under leaves. Just a glimpse and it was gone. He turned over and checked his sense-lines, but the countryside was empty except for the numb minds of sheep, and the faint intelligences of the listening oaks, too deep and old for him to reach.

Next day, for hours, they climbed the relentless ridge. Each time Raffi was sure they had finally sweated to the top, another fold of hill would rise up before them, and the bitter wind flapped their coats and rippled the long wet grass. The hills were empty; few animals lived here and fewer trees, only stunted shreds of old hedgerow, sheep-gnawed and bare, and the immense burrows of ridge-rats, the fat females scattering from under their feet.

Clouds swept over, some dragging showers. Soon they were soaked, Raffi was glad of his coat. Turning the collar up, he smelt suddenly, as if it were real, a scent of soap, of woodsmoke. Ahead of him Galen limped grimly, finding ruts and tracks in the slippery grass; the Sekoi stalked far behind, its fur drenched, miserably silent.

Just below the ridge, Galen stopped. He turned quickly and stared out at the grey country below, blurred by showers.

The Sekoi walked past him. 'Come on, keeper.'

'Wait.' Galen was alert, his eyes dark. 'Do you feel that, Raffi?'

Raffi opened his third eye, groping into distance.

115

Far at the edge of his mind-sight, something rippled. 'Men?' he said doubtfully.

'Men. Following us.'

The Sekoi had stopped; now it came slithering back in alarm. 'Are you sure?'

'Certain.' The keeper glanced round hastily. 'Over there. We're too exposed.'

They ran to the hollow and slid in; the bottom was muddy and sheep-trodden. As Galen rummaged in the pack, Raffi knelt up and stared out; the land seemed empty, but he knew Galen's sense-lines were stronger than his, reaching far into stone and soil. The keeper had tugged out the seeing-tube, one of their most precious relics; as he murmured the prayer of humility and gazed through it the Sekoi looked on with interest. Its yellow eyes flickered to Raffi.

'A relic?'

'It makes far-off things seem nearer.'

'Got them,' Galen muttered. He was rigid a moment, the tube pointing north-east into a brief moving patch of sunlight on a distant slope. 'Ten. Eleven. All on horseback.'

'The Watch,' Raffi said.

'I don't think so.' Galen's voice was sour; he lowered the tube. 'Take a look.'

Eagerly, Raffi took the relic and held it to his eye, touching the red button so that the blurred circle suddenly shrivelled into focus, and he saw trees, small in the distance, and between them horses running, red-painted.

'Alberic?' the Sekoi said to Galen.

'Without doubt.'

'But how could he be so close?'

'Godric must have been meeting him near by. He wasn't worried about having to take you any distance, was he?'

Across the circle a shape flashed: Raffi steadied the tube, brought it back, carefully. The rider was tiny, muffled in coats; turning, shouting something.

'It's him,' he muttered.

'Besides,' Galen said acidly, 'they probably asked at some cottage.'

Raffi scowled, watching the minute horseman vanish behind trees. He gave the tube back curtly, and after a second's hesitation Galen offered it to the Sekoi.

The creature's eyes glinted; it held the tube carefully with its fourteen long fingers, then lifted it and looked in, and its whole body quivered with surprise.

'I see them,' it said after a moment. 'They're riding fast. They'll be here in less than an hour.' It looked round, anxiously. 'They'll catch us.'

'Maybe.' Galen took the relic and stowed it away. 'Come on.'

They hurried to the ridge-top. The gale increased, pushing them back; Raffi felt he was struggling with a great invisible force, coming out of the land ahead, a hostile force, something he had never felt before. 'What is it?' he gasped.

Galen gave him a sideways look. 'We're coming to the end, boy.'

'The end?' For a moment he thought that the ridge was the edge of the world, that there was some vast giddy chasm on the other side, but as Galen hauled him up over the rocks and the full rage of the wind crashed against them, making him stagger over the skyline, he saw what the keeper meant.

They had indeed come to the end.

For in front of them were the Unfinished Lands.

14

*Out of the Pit came disease. For leagues
around, the trees died; grasses curled.
Unseasonal frosts split the rocks. The
Makers abandoned their works. In
Tasceron they brooded on the treachery
of Kest.*

Book of the Seven Moons

It was the wreckage of a world.

The hill that Raffi stood on descended into
swamp, a green decaying morass stretching as far
as he could see, humped and hollowed, dissolving
into poisonous yellow mist. Thunder cracked and
rumbled; at the horizon were vast jagged ranges,
as if mountains had surged up and shattered into
sharp slopes. Even the weather was evil: an icy,
spitting rain.

The Sekoi shivered. 'Chaos creeps in on us.'

'Indeed it does.' Galen stood upright in the chill
wind, staring out. 'Year by year the Unfinished
Lands creep back, undoing the Makers' works.
Spreading like a disease.'

'I see no island out there, keeper.'

Galen looked over. 'Nor do I.'

'Will it not have been destroyed, like the rest?'

'Maybe.' He stared again into the mist. 'But I
believe it is there, somewhere. Hard to find.
Dangerous. If you don't share that faith, I won't
blame you if you don't come.'

Raffi watched them both. The Sekoi rubbed
sleet from its furred face. It glanced back up the

118

hillside. Then it shrugged, unhappy. 'I'll come. For the moment.'

'We'll find it.' Abruptly Galen stalked off down the slope.

The Sekoi stared after him. 'I'm glad you're so sure,' it muttered.

Half an hour later, the stink of the mere choking him, Raffi leaned on a rock to catch his breath. They were at the bottom of the slope. Already the ground was soft, oozing with water. 'I thought this was moorland?' he gasped.

'Swallowed up.' Galen stabbed the mire with his stick. 'Kest's work, all of this. Once he began to meddle with the world, changing things, no one could stop it. Only the Order fought to keep the balance, kept it so for centuries. But since the Watch destroyed us, all that's lost.'

'It makes you wonder,' Raffi said suddenly, looking up. 'What if the Watch is Kest's work too?'

Galen's glance turned him cold, stabbed him. He felt the shock of it, the tingle of power that he knew was some stirring of the Crow. For an instant the scream of migrating birds rang like alien voices. Galen's eyes were sharp and dark. But all he said was, 'I sometimes think so.'

'Relicmaster!'

The yell made them turn.

A row of horses stood on the hillcrest, high above. From the central one a small figure was grinning down at them. 'How are you, Galen Harn?' he called, his voice ringing among the rocks.

The Sekoi spat, and snarled something in its own language.

'Keep still,' Galen muttered. Then he called back, 'I'm well, thief-lord. But you're too far from home.'

119

Alberic's warband smirked; one of them said something and they all laughed. Raffi let his sense-lines play over them; he felt weapons, a ruthless confidence. They weren't worried.

Alberic waved an arm at the marsh. 'You seem to be running into trouble.' He was wearing a coat of quilted blue satin and bearskin, his small, clever face mocking. 'Nowhere left to go.'

'I go where I'd planned to go,' Galen growled.

'Really? Well I'd hate to see that little blue death-box of mine sinking in a swamp. Why not leave it behind for me?'

'Come down and get it.'

Alberic shook his head. Even from here Raffi could see the glint in his bright, hooded eyes. 'I intend to. Or at least my boys and girls here will come down. I don't like blood on my clothes.'

Galen folded his arms. It was a small action, but Alberic's grin faded. He frowned out at the marsh. 'I hope you're not going to be stupid.'

Galen laughed, his rare, harsh laugh. It terrified Raffi, and he knew at once it had worried the dwarf.

'I'm walking out into chaos, little man,' the keeper said grimly. 'And if it drags me down all the relics go with me. I'd rather the swamp had them than leave them with you. You're a disgrace to your kind, thief-lord. Your soul is shrivelled like a plumstone. You're forgetting how to feel, how to know joy. You're tired of all the world, Alberic, and the more you get the more it turns to ashes in your hand.'

For a moment they watched each other, unmoving, the dwarf's face set and cold. Then Galen turned. 'Come on.'

They scrambled into the soft, yielding swamp.

Behind them Alberic stood up in his saddle, furious. 'Keeper! Don't be a fool!'

'Keep going,' Galen snapped. 'Don't look back.'

An arrow slashed the reeds. The soft ground vibrated with hoof-beats; Raffi felt them as he thrust aside the tall reeds.

'Boy! Are you going to follow him to your death?' Alberic's yell was raw with anger; Raffi tried to ignore it, but his foot sank suddenly into the mud and he plunged with a gasp, up to his waist.

Galen tugged him up. 'Keep hold of me!'

'It's deep!'

'It'll get deeper.'

In front of them the Sekoi slithered in, its face squirming with distaste. Raffi floundered, his boots deep in the mud, the green stinking mire giving off reeks and vapours that made him dizzy. Great weeds clustered over him, giant scumwort with its hairy leaves like hands on his hair and neck. As Galen moved ahead, Raffi slipped and fell, this time right under the murky water.

He yelled, then choked. Hands hauled him out; a sudden swirl of the mist showed him Godric's face, grinning, and he squirmed and fought but they had him, they were dragging him away, three of them, and somewhere Alberic was shouting orders, his voice pitched high.

'Galen!' he screamed. He kicked but his legs were grabbed. A muddy hand slammed over his mouth but he yelled again with all his mind-power, at the keeper, at the Makers, and at the same time a blue shaft of light slashed past him; the knot of men leapt apart in terror.

'The box!' Alberic raged. 'He's using my box!'

Raffi picked himself up. A horse's hooves almost trampled him; looking up through a sudden tear in the fog, he glimpsed the girl, Sikka, her snake-armour glinting. She saw him and shouted; then he was up, floundering, and Galen was somewhere close pulling him by some strong mind-tug so that he hurtled into the marsh in a shower of arrows and sank deep, only his face above water, splashing, drowning, till a hand grabbed his tight and Galen's voice said, 'Quiet!'

Instantly, the night was very still.

Two slow bubbles oozed from below and plipped, one by one, under his ear.

Silence slapped in ripples against the scumwort stalks.

When Alberic spoke, they were shocked at how close he sounded. 'All right, Galen. You've made your point. It's noble, but what good are drowned bodies? Is that what the Makers would want?'

Harness creaked in the fog.

The dwarf's voice was calm, reassuring. 'Come out. We'll talk terms.'

Galen's mouth came close to Raffi's ear. 'Walk. Slowly. Don't splash.'

'Where?' Raffi breathed.

'Out there.'

'There's nothing for you out there, keeper!' It was as if Alberic had heard them. Now he was barely controlling his fury. 'You'll drown, or the fog will choke you! There are horrors out there, Galen, fish that will eat your fingers away, steel-worms, leeches, grubs that burrow into the flesh. Nothing else! And you, Cat-creature, water-hater, you know I'm right! The Great Hoard will never have that gold that's weighing you down!'

Near by in the fog, the Sekoi sighed. 'The worst thing is, he's right.'

'Ignore him.' Galen led the way, carefully

brushing through leaves. They waded after him, trying not to make a sound.

'Gnats will lay their eggs in your hair, keeper! Germs, hideous fevers, that's all you'll get. I want that box! Give me that and you can go, all of you!'

He was raging now, desperate.

In grim silence Galen waded always deeper, the scumwort dark above them. Insects whined. On a sudden open stretch of water Raffi saw the pale moon, Agramon, like a coin on black cloth.

'Galen!' Alberic's roar was distant now. 'Are you that scared of me?'

But they were far out, and the swamp was up to Raffi's chin, so that if he stumbled it washed into his ears and he swallowed it, coughing and spitting. He gripped tight on to the keeper's coat, and the night closed in around them, until they were struggling and hacking their way through the stiff growths, gasping for breath, bitten by innumerable flies.

In no time at all he was exhausted. His drenched clothes dragged him down; the relentless suction of the mud made every step an effort. He was coughing, half-choked by the marsh vapour. So was the Sekoi, its thin bedraggled shoulders barely visible, shuddering uncontrollably with the bitter cold.

The water swirled. Something nibbled Raffi's knee; he panicked, jerking and splashing, yelling in fear.

Galen grabbed him. 'What!'

'It was biting me!' He held on, shaking.

'There's nothing there.'

'It'll be back!' The Sekoi's snarl shocked them; it was a hiss of despair. Looming up in the mist they saw its yellow eyes, the short fur swollen with bites and tics. 'For Flains' sake, Galen! We have to go back!'

Stubborn, the keeper shook his soaked hair. 'We're close,' he gasped. 'I know we're close.'

'There's nothing out here!' The creature came close to him, clasped his arm with its spindly, dripping fingers. 'Nothing! It's all gone. The Unfinished Lands have spread over it. Even if we get to the island it will be overgrown, stinking, poisoned. Listen to me. All this is folly. We can get back, avoid Alberic, get clear. We can still be safe . . .'

Its voice was low, hypnotic. Tingles of warning hummed in Raffi's mind; he knew it was putting them under the story-spell but he didn't care, he wanted that, to convince Galen, to get them all out before his strength went, before . . .

'NO!' Galen's roar was savage. A sudden burst of energy sparked in Raffi; he stumbled, flung an arm out wildly to stop himself going under. He struck something hard. Solid.

'It won't work on me!' the keeper yelled.

'Galen,' Raffi breathed.

'Go back if you want to! Take the boy! I'll walk to my death before I give up!'

'Then walk to it!' the Sekoi snarled. 'This isn't faith. It's stupidity!'

Raffi put out his other hand and felt the structure. It was real. Marshlight flickered cold phosphorescent flames under it.

'Galen.'

'*What*?' the keeper roared.

'There's some sort of trackway . . .'

In the hush an eelworm rippled by his face. Then the water surged, and Galen pushed him aside.

It was a mesh of branches, woven tight, rammed down between uprights. Old, oozing into decay. But in the green fumes of the fog it was a godsend.

Galen hauled off the sodden pack and dumped it in the Sekoi's arms. Then he put up his hands and climbed, tugging himself up in a great heave of water. Branches cracked; mist closed about him. Something bit Raffi's cheek and he slapped at it, his whole body shuddering.

Then Galen was leaning down, eyes bright, dark hair falling forward. 'Come on.'

Dragged up, Raffi felt himself dumped on the mesh of branches; he collapsed there, lying still, letting the water run from him endlessly, pouring out of his hair and sleeves and pockets, out of his eyes, out of his mind. He didn't know he had blacked out until Galen grabbed him, propped him up, rubbing his soaked arms briskly. 'No time to sleep. You'll freeze.'

Shivering, he nodded. Now that they were out of the water the cold was unbearable; he couldn't stop shaking.

Galen pulled him upright. 'This trackway leads somewhere,' he said harshly, 'and we need to find out where.'

He was elated. Numbly, Raffi felt it, and wondered why. In all the stillness of the fog, all the endless miles of marsh there was nothing his mind could touch, no one, no Maker-power, nothing but a nightmare of swimming, slithering things, and all the threads of power that should have been in the land were tangled, broken, deeply drowned. But Galen was fierce with hope; he hardly waited for them, forcing his way through the leaves, then walking swiftly, carelessly over the creaking, splitting mesh of the trackway.

The Sekoi pushed Raffi on. 'I sometimes think his mind's gone,' it muttered bitterly. 'That business in the city. It scorched him.'

Raffi shook his head, dragging himself over a

hole. 'He's always been like this. Even before he spoke to the Makers. This is why they chose him.'

The Sekoi was silent. The trackway led them deeper into murk; at times they could hardly see each other. Galen was a shadow far ahead. Raffi was stumbling; he felt sick and ill, hot and thirsty and bitterly cold all at once.

And then he saw that Galen had stopped.

The keeper stood still. Very still. Crowding behind, Raffi saw they had come to the end of the trackway. It broke off abruptly, and beyond it was nothing. Nothing but fog.

The Sekoi gave a hiss of despair. Raffi clutched his hands to fists. He wanted to sink down and cry, but he wouldn't, he wouldn't. He was a scholar of the Order. He had to have faith.

Into the silence the Sekoi said, 'What now?'

Galen didn't answer. He was alert, as if he listened.

'Perhaps it's at the other end,' Raffi muttered hopelessly.

'No it's not.' Galen gripped his stick tight. 'It's here.'

And before they could stop him he stepped out, into the marsh.

Raffi yelled, grabbed, but to his amazement the keeper didn't sink; he stood there, on the scummy surface, as if it were solid, something real and hard.

And instantly everything changed.

A warm breeze blew the fog apart. He smelt grass, and apples, and to his astonishment the moons came out one by one above him, as if they had been waiting there all the time.

Before them, dark grass sloped in the moonlight, and a figure was sitting under the apple trees.

When she stood up, they saw she had two shadows, each an echo of herself.

'Welcome, keepers,' she said, and smiled. 'I was afraid there was no one left to come.'

15

There no trouble will be;
There the summer will linger.
There I will speak to my people
with the water's tongue.

Flain to Artelan, Artelan's Dream

He was awake but he didn't open his eyes.

Instead he lay curled in the warm heavy fleeces, completely relaxed, hearing somewhere outside the trickle of water over stones, an endless liquid ripple. Behind that was birdsong, a robin or pine-finch, and beyond that, silence, a tranquil silence with no worry.

He dozed again, but the oily wool tickled his bare shoulders. Scratching, he rolled, yawned, opened his eyes. Then he sat up.

The house was large and pillared, swept clean, the door open, letting sunlight in. Raffi fingered the bites on his face. It was afternoon; he'd slept too long.

Getting up he found his clothes, washed, amazingly soft; as he pulled them on he tried to remember the last time they had been clean, and couldn't. He splashed in a silver bowl of water, soaking his hair and neck. As he dried himself, the Sekoi's shadow darkened the doorway. 'So you're awake!' It looked cheerful, despite a swollen eyelid.

'Where's Galen?'

'Near. He hasn't slept much. Spent most of the morning talking with Tallis.'

Raffi frowned. He had only glimpsed the woman last night, had felt a great sense of age, a bent figure in the dark. 'Is she the only one here?'

The Sekoi grinned and winked at him. 'She's the Guardian. Whether there's only one of her I haven't worked out yet.' And it went back out, bending under the low door.

Puzzled, he followed it.

Outside, he stared around in a sudden warmth of delight. The house stood among green lawns, studded with ancient oaks and calarna trees, and beyond were apple orchards; even from here he could smell the ripening fruit. Near him were phlox and high banks of overripe daisies and some red gentians still in flower, and foxgloves with the fat bees fumbling in their speckled bells. The sky was blue and warm. Beyond the trees, a strange hill rose up almost to a point, an eerie humped outcrop with a buzzard circling over it, just as Artelan might have seen it in his dream.

The Sekoi was grinning at him. 'Hard to believe, little keeper?'

'How is it here? How has it survived?'

It shrugged. 'Ask the Guardian. It seems the Order has more power left than my people thought.'

Galen was sprawled on the grass, under a calarna tree. He looked oddly clean too, wearing a green shirt, and on his face was a look of grave content that Raffi had not seen there before. Beside him was a woman. She stood up, stiffly, and he saw she was very old; a small, bent woman in a russet dress, her hair white, her face shrewd and wrinkled.

'Welcome, Raffi. Have something to eat.'

'Thanks.' He crouched down at the half-empty plates, littered with cuts of ham and cheeses and crusty bread that broke white and soft. There were different fruits too, currants and pears, and hot pies full of blackberries, and jugs of cream. Relentlessly, he began to eat.

They watched him for a while. Then Galen said, 'When will I begin?'

'Tomorrow.' The woman's eyes, palest blue, watched Raffi in amusement.

'Begin what?' he muttered, swallowing.

'The Ordeals.' She looked out at the orchard. 'Galen has told me why you've come. To find out where this child, this Interrex, is, he will have to drink from the spring, and that needs preparation if it is to be safe. A time of fasting, of prayer, the pilgrimage of repentance round the island, a night alone on the peak. Then, when he's ready, he will drink.'

Raffi cut himself a big slice of pie. 'How long will it take?'

Galen shifted, the awen-beads shining. 'That depends on the Makers.'

'And on you,' the woman said softly.

He nodded. 'Yes. On me. We may be keepers, Guardian, but life outside has changed us. The teachings are in fragments and we've lost so much. Too many days spent running and hiding, not in prayer. Too few relics. And the Maker-life in the trees and leaves and stones curling up, harder to reach.'

For a moment she watched him. 'It hurts you,' she said.

He glanced up, eyes dark. 'Yes. But this place . . . here the life is strong. How have you kept it?'

The Sekoi came and sat down, its long fingers picking at the damsons. She nodded at it. 'Our friend here has a belt full of gold coins wound about his body.'

The Sekoi almost choked.

Raffi laughed aloud. 'How did you know?'

'Oh, I know. But he keeps his treasure hidden, under the surface, and so do we, here. Flain made this island holy. The ground has deep lines of energy, the water strange properties. While the swamp spread round us, year by year, we worried, but the island has stayed untouched. Some keepers still came in the troubled years, we heard what was happening: the Fall of Tasceron, the Emperor's death. But the swamp thickened and fog rose out of it and we were lost. The Watch never found us.'

Raffi rubbed a finger round his empty plate. Into the silence he said, 'Us?'

Tallis looked at him, her smile sharp. 'Did I say us? There's only me.'

She tried to stand then, stiffly, and Galen had to help her. When he crouched to collect the dishes, her gnarled hand caught his shoulder. 'No. You prepare yourself, keeper. The boy will help me – in return I will give him his lessons, while you're busy.'

Galen nodded gratefully. 'He needs it. Work him hard.'

She met Raffi's eyes and smiled. 'Oh, I will.'

But after the dishes were clean she let him go exploring, wandering through the long grass of the orchards. The branches were heavy with apples, russets and pippins and medlars falling into rotten, wasp-tunnelled softness in the grass. The air was rich with scent and the buzz of honey-bees. At the end of the fields was a gate, and coming through that he found himself on a track, green and over-grown, the tall umbels of burrwort and hemlock and hare's-ear turning to heads of seed and fluff that drifted in the slightest breeze. Birds whistled; from the elm trees a few leaves pattered, caught on webs, spinning. It was so warm he took his jacket off and hung it on the hedge and walked on, humming, wondering at how happy he felt. It was as if they had stepped out of some endless heartbreak. Here, time stopped. Nothing could get in.

He left the track at a stile and began to climb the hill, quickly at first and then more slowly, the sweat cooling on him, the breeze whipping his hair. Soon his chest thudded with the steepness; he dragged in huge breaths, labouring on, and whenever he looked up the smooth green slopes hung out over him, so steep he almost had to pull himself up with his hands.

When he scrambled over the top he was breathless; soaked with sweat, he crumpled in the spiky grass. Below him the island lay warm in the evening light. Beyond orchards and woodland the sun was setting; a great red globe shimmering in the cloudbanks, the strange shifting veils of mist that hid the marsh. He watched it sink, breathing deep, fingering the blue and purple awen-beads. This was how it should be, how it had been. This was the rule of the Order, all that Galen was fighting for. Odd memories moved through his mind. Slowly, over hours, the colour drained; the island became a purple twilight of moths and owls calling from the distant woods. He stared down at it, still, unmoving.

That night Galen lit the log fire in the house, and the candles were arranged. The Sekoi watched, curious. 'Can I stay?'

'If you want,' Galen said drily. 'You might learn something.'

Two of the cats that lived there came in over the windowledge; one climbed warmly on to the Sekoi's lap, curling itself up, the other coming and purring at its ear. The creature purred back, as if it spoke to them. Then it said, 'I apologize for my behaviour in the marsh. You were right, as we see.'

For a moment Galen's hand was still. Then he lit another candle. 'This time,' he said quietly.

Raffi turned as the door opened. To his amazement, a young woman came in, with long red hair braided and loose. She sat down next to Galen.

'Are we ready?'

'When you are, Guardian.'

She glanced across, archly. 'Raffi?'

They were grinning at him, he knew. He tried not to look bewildered. 'I'm ready.'

So they sat, the three of them, and Tallis began, because he knew it was her, the same woman, somehow impossibly younger. In a shimmer of candles and bells they chanted the long, sonorous verses of the Litany, the praises of the Makers, and it sounded more mysterious to Raffi than ever before, until Galen and Tallis went on into chants and chapters he hadn't learned yet, full of the sorrows of the broken world and the echoes of ancient words.

Later, when he slept in the warm bed, the words ran through his head, endless as the rippling water outside.

On Sarres, day blurred into day. Scarlet calarna leaves fell silently into the grass. Galen fasted, and spent long hours meditating in the quiet garden, as still as if he slept. On the second day he walked barefoot up the hill; from below Raffi watched him, sprawled in the warm sun. They prayed the prayers together, morning and sunset, and then Raffi had lessons from Tallis, or fed the hens, or helped pick the endless crop of apples and pears.

Tallis bewildered him. Sometimes she was old,

and sometimes a woman of about twenty, her red hair swinging, full of energy, climbing the apple ladders and whistling. And once, as he fished in the narrow lake for carp, he saw her come out of the trees and call him, and he sat up, cold, because now she was a little girl, barely ten, her voice high and petulant.

'It's time to come in for tea.'

He stood. She was small, her face plump, her red hair tangled. The russet dress was short, showed bare legs.

'Who are you?' he breathed. 'How can you do this?'

The little girl grinned. 'I'm the Guardian,' she said. Then she put out her tongue at him and ran away.

He asked the Sekoi about it, because Galen was too busy. The creature had made a hammock for itself between trees in the orchard; it spent hours here, slumbering in the shade, lazily.

Now it fanned itself with a chestnut leaf, one leg dangling. 'You're the keeper.'

'But I don't understand! Is she ... have the Makers given her this ability? Which age is she really?'

'Really is a word with no meaning.' The Sekoi closed its eyes. 'My people have stories of similar beings. After all, we all have our past ages somewhere inside of us.'

Raffi picked a stone out of the grass and turned it over. 'You mean she's not human?'

'Why not? I'm not.'

'Yes, but ... well, there's your people and ours. That's all.'

'And the Crow?'

He glanced up; the Sekoi was looking at him with one eye open.

'What?'

'What I mean is, small keeper, the Makers re-made this world and then Kest warped it. Who knows what beings are here?'

Raffi thought about that for a while. Then he said, 'I'd like to live in this place for ever.'

But either it was asleep, gently rocking, or it had no answer for him.

Next day he was memorizing Artelan's dream when he looked up at her. She was sewing the tears in his coat, so old now, her face drawn and wrinkled, her hands stiff, knobbly with arthritis. 'Tell me about the Well,' he said. 'In all the time we've been here I've never seen it.'

'All the time?' she mocked, gently. 'How long is that, do you think?'

'Six days. Seven?'

'Four.'

He was astonished. 'Is that all?'

She brushed wisps of grey hair off her cheek. He saw how the skin sagged in folds under her chin. 'That's all. As for the spring, it's not far. You can hear it, can't you?'

'I've heard it since we came.'

'If you want to find it you can. And Galen will be ready soon.' She looked at him, her eyes pale. 'Your master is a strange man. Something has entered him.'

He looked back at the tattered book in his lap. 'I know.'

Watching him, she said, 'A man hard to live with?'

'He always was.' And he lay down on his back in the grass and closed his eyes, laying the book on his chest.

Later, after supper, he went out across the dim lawns, following the ripple of water. Behind him in the house Tallis sang in her little-girl voice, and the Sekoi lounged by the fire, joining in tunelessly. He didn't know where Galen was.

The evening was purple, faintly misty. Far off three moons hung, Cyrax, Karnos, Lar, the last a pale crescent nearly setting. Stars glinted in the branches. Everything was so still that his feet sounded loud in the grass, the low branches he brushed aside sharp rustles and cracks.

The ripple was louder. It sounded like a voice now, an endless song of secrets and lost lore. He pushed under a thick yew, and found that its huge ancient trunk grew out from a mass of splintered rock, and beneath it the water ran from a deep crack, falling into a small pool edged with mossy stones. Chained to the brink was a silver cup, lying on its side.

He squatted and touched the water. It was cold, and looked black. A few dead leaves floated on the surface and he picked them off. Then, without thinking, he picked the cup up and filled it, seeing the seven moon-sigils of the Order on its side, almost worn smooth from the wear of hands that had used it.

The water rippled and splashed into the pool.

He knew he shouldn't do this, that he hadn't prepared, but it was only water, only a sip, and he was so thirsty all at once, and if something happened, really happened, then Galen might be pleased that he could do it, that he was fit to be a real keeper.

He put the cup to his lips, and drank.

It was cold.

Once he'd begun, he couldn't stop until it was empty.

16

To make the Deep Journey the keeper
must be ready, and of age.
He must have completed the Ordeals, and
be wise.
Or else his mind will shatter in the grip
of the Makers.

> Fourth Warning of Gaeraint

He was flying.
Though he had no wings.
No body.

Giddily he stared down through the fleeting clouds; they sped under him, and plunging through their rifts and tears he saw a whole countryside spread out below; green fields, hedges, the long unwinding glitter of rivers, then a sudden upsurge of mountains, so that the air iced, and he gasped and soared into cloud, through tiny crystals sharp as needles, and then out again, sunwarmed, the frost on his eyelashes melting.

He fought for control, but couldn't stop, couldn't hold himself steady. Below now were networks of lakes and a great forest; the smell of sap and pine dizzied him, the trees seemed to shout at him. He plunged down, crashing through the treetops and all the birds flew out, screaming irritation; jekkles yelled and chattered. Dragged out, breathless, upside down, he air-tumbled over fields, bare and furrowed, struggling to slow down, until he steadied and looked on the ground for his speeding shadow, and it wasn't there.

He knew what this was. This was the Ride, the first part of the Deep Journey, and it would go on and on for ever unless he could control it. A swarm of mere-bees flashed around him; he squirmed, stung, screamed for it to stop. Next he tried closing his eyes, fighting for mind-control, but that was worse; he couldn't breathe, was terrified of flying smack into some hill. Opening his eyes he gave a stifled screech, and was sucked into a narrow crack in a mountainside, buffeted along it, dragged through an icy chasm so that the rock walls grazed him, banging and bruising, seeing close up the astonished eyes of a fire-fox in a cave, tiny green lichens, the twist of a snake that fell from its ledge and plunged past him in a rattle of stones.

Abruptly a rock reared ahead; he cried out and jerked aside and he was out! He was out in a wide blue sky and he yelled in relief and caught hold of his mind, slowing himself, slowing, fighting bitterly for control.

He dropped, carefully. Now he had it; then it all slipped away and he was plunging wildly again through endless blue air. He couldn't keep it up. Panicking, he held on, praying for help, gabbling the Litany in terror over and over.

He was above the Unfinished Lands. They were more terrible than he had dreamed. Below were vast plateaux where nothing grew, where great cracks had opened in the ground, and plumes of filthy smoke hissed up and choked him. Flames and sparks spat from ravines; ahead a cone of ash erupted scorching lava, its grey cinderfield spreading destruction for miles. Briefly he saw ruins, crushed houses. Beyond that the land heaved and buckled as he watched, as if the very atoms of rock and soil were coming undone; convulsions cracked mountains, new rivers gushed out, sinister lichens crawled over every rotting growth. He began to think he was soaring over some great disease, as if Anara was pocked and pustuled with abscesses, as if the planet burned and tossed in fever, and then below him, coming suddenly into view, was the worst of it, a great wound, a vast open sore in the planet's side, and out of it crawled creatures so disfigured that even from this height they filled him with horror.

These were the Pits of Maar.

Seven great holes, like some obscene reversal of the moons.

They were in every story he'd ever heard, and the sight of them filled him with dread. The nearest was pulling at him. Desperately he struggled to tug away, but it had him, it dragged him and he tipped over and fell, head first, mile after mile, arms out, screaming. Below, the Pit gaped, spiralling down in immense terraces, thousands of them, one beneath the other, and as he fell into it the darkness closed round him, and swallowed him in one gulp.

He was standing in a room.

It was very dark; there were no candles. A small fire burned in a brazier, and as Raffi looked he saw that in front of it was a desk, and at the desk, far back in the shadows, someone was writing.

Bewildered, he stared around. He felt sick and giddy, battered, sore, and for a moment the room seemed to sway around him, and then it was still.

There was no sound but the pen, scratching.

He was glad of the fire; awkwardly he stretched out his hands to it and saw with a shock that they were frail and ghostly, and he could see right through them.

The figure that was writing never turned its

head, but quite suddenly the scratch of the pen was an ominous sound, as if the words it formed were evil words, and Raffi knew that the writer had sensed him, or heard him. He kept still, his heart thumping.

It was too dark to see the figure properly, but there was a wrongness about it, a slither of soft mesh or scales, something abhorrent in the shape. Slowly, it stopped writing, and put down the pen.

Raffi stared, astonished, at the hand that lay in the firelight. It was long, ridged. Unhuman.

And then he knew, suddenly and surely, that he was in the very depths of hell, in the Pits of Maar, and that for mile upon mile above him the unimaginable horrors of Kest bred and spawned and crawled.

The figure spoke. Its voice was low, reptilian. 'Who are you?' it hissed.

Rigid with terror, Raffi couldn't answer.

He could see the edge of its face: long, too long. If it got up and walked into the firelight he knew he would collapse, crumple in on himself, that it would destroy his mind like a searing flame. But he couldn't take his eyes off it.

Close your eyes, he screamed at himself. Close your eyes! But they were fixed. The eyelids were heavy sheets of steel; he couldn't do it, couldn't force them down.

The figure stirred.

'A keeper!' it said, wondering. It began to stand.

And then, abruptly, Galen was there, Galen was helping him. Together they forced down the iron blinds, blotting out room, fire, the nightmare narrow turning face. But Raffi was screaming, or someone was, far off, over and over, and for a second he saw himself lying in a dark bed, and the tall shapes were holding him down and calling him, calling him.

There was a hundred years of silence.

Water dripped into a pool.

'Raffi?'

Ages later, Carys was standing with him. They were alone in a golden place. She looked round, bewildered. 'Where are we?'

He was sitting on a stone, huddled up. When she spoke he found he could move, stiffly, could rub his face with his hands. His skin felt strange, his hands like an old man's.

'I don't know.'

She knelt and caught hold of his arm. 'Are you all right?'

'I'm glad you're here.'

'But where's here? And I wish that screaming would stop!'

Vaguely, he thought he could do something about that. Far off, he let it ebb into silence. Then he said, 'This is all a dream. A vision. I drank the water of the well, Carys. I shouldn't have done that. It was so stupid! And now I'm lost. I don't know where I am; I've been here too long. And I can't get back!'

She looked at him closely. 'You look older. You *are* older.'

He knew that, could feel himself ageing, as if month by month all his years were speeding up inside him. His chin felt stubbly, his hands too big.

She caught hold of him, and her hands were warm. 'Concentrate, Raffi! What did you come here for?'

'What?'

Impatient, she shook him. 'What are you looking for? Is it the Interrex?'

'Yes!'

Suddenly the word shone in front of him; he reached out his hands and caught hold of it and it was solid, heavy. It was a box, and he opened it and climbed inside, and walked down the long stairway. Behind him, Carys stood on the top step.

'Hurry up!' she hissed. 'Time's running out!'

He could see it too, time trickling down the stairs past him like water, rippling and dripping, the sound loud and close, a spring that never ran dry.

By the bottom of the stairs he was old; his hair was white and he couldn't straighten; a pain throbbed in his side. But as he limped on, a sense-line came out of the dark and wrapped itself around him, and instantly he was young, only about ten, and he opened a door and walked into the classroom.

It was a huge room. Bitterly cold.

About fifty children sat there in rows, writing in utter silence, and he realized with a shock they were all wearing round their necks the insignia of the Watch.

He slid into a desk at the back, picked up the pen and read what was on the paper. It was Galen's handwriting.

Which one of them is the Interrex?

Glancing up, he saw a tall lean man patrolling the lanes between desks, a splintered stick under his arm. Every now and then he would stop and bark out a number. A child shot up, instantly, chanted a section of the Rule, and sat down.

Something cold touched Raffi's chest. Feeling

142

inside his shirt, he pulled out a small metal disc
on a chain and read the number on it.

914

Then he noticed, on the opposite side of the
room, a small girl, her red hair hacked short. She
was no more than six or seven, and was watching
him slyly. He smiled at her.

Instantly her hand shot up.

'What?' the Watchmaster roared.

'He isn't writing.'

'Who isn't?'

'Him.'

She pointed. Every head turned to Raffi. He
swallowed; the Watchmaster was already striding
down the aisle like a great long-legged stork.

'Stand up,' he hissed.

It really was a stork now, a black one with a
viciously sharp beak. 'Speak the Rule,' it snapped,
but Raffi didn't know the words.

The bird's beak jabbed his chest. 'Speak!'

'I . . . I can't.'

'Can't?'

'I don't know it,' he shouted, desperate. Then
he glared across at the girl. 'Why did you tell him?'

She giggled. 'The Watch must watch each other
first, stupid.'

Raffi. Can you hear me?

'He's a spy!' the stork hissed.

They were all around him now, crowding, prod-
ding. They held him tight, he couldn't move, and
though they were children they were changing
before his eyes, slithering, growing tails, mutating
with nightmare speed.

'He must be punished!' The stork beak stabbed
at his eyes; he jerked aside in terror. 'Where is
this?' he yelled. 'What Watchhouse? Tell me!'

Raffi.

The girl smirked, her ears pointed like a cat's. 'Keilder Wood 770.'

Raffi! He's coming. He's coming!

Hands scratched at him; he fought and bit and struggled but they had him and the vicious beak stabbed at his forehead till the pain exploded in him and the blood ran down, and a voice was saying over and over, 'Raffi. Don't fight us, Raffi. Open your eyes. Open your eyes.'

And finally, hopelessly, though he knew they were open, he opened them.

The Sekoi sat back, weary and gaunt with relief. 'It's all right, Galen,' it muttered. 'He's back.'

17

'I can't believe,' Galen growled, 'that you were stupid enough to do it.'

Tallis and the Sekoi exchanged glances. 'Never mind that now.' She pressed the warm cup into Raffi's hands. 'It's all over, at last.'

The room was dark. They were sitting round the fire, Tallis in her young woman shape, the door behind her open, so they could see the moths in the soft moonlight over the lawns.

Raffi sipped the warm ale. He still felt tired and guilty and dizzy. Yesterday they'd told him he'd been in the dream-coma for three days and nights. He knew now he'd never have got out of it on his own; Galen had come in for him, in deep, into the journey, because that's what it had been, the Deep Journey that only Relicmasters should make. It would have killed him soon. Even now, a whole day later, he barely had the strength to make a sense-line, and fell over if he stood up.

The ale was honey-sweet. It made him feel better.

When he had woken, all he had wanted to do was be sick, and then sleep. But Galen had been relentless. He had forced him to tell the dream, all of it, every detail, before he had let him collapse into nausea. Now the keeper sat grim, his hooked face dark and shadowed.

'I'm sorry,' Raffi muttered. It sounded weak, and stupid. 'I just ... I didn't think anything would happen to me.'

'You didn't think at all.' Galen was haggard and weary; all his fasting had made him thinner, and Raffi knew he had prayed over him and fought with him for control all the time of the dream-sleep. 'It was a mess, boy,' he said fiercely. 'You could have ruined everything.'

'But he hasn't, it seems.' Tallis put in smoothly. She sat down on the floor, her back against the bench. 'And now we must discuss these messages the Makers have sent. However they came.'

The Sekoi put a bony finger into its ale-cup and stirred, thoughtfully. 'Odd messages, too. And dispiriting.' It looked up. 'The last part seems the most important for us. Do you agree that it seems to tell us that the Interrex is a small girl-cub, and that she is in the hands of the Watch? In a Watch-house?'

Galen nodded gloomily.

'You mean that girl who put her hand up?' Raffi went cold. 'She's the Emperor's granddaughter? But she's one of the enemy!'

Tallis shook her head. 'It may be her. It may be the number round your neck will be more important. 914. Remember it. At least we have a clear idea where to look. Keilder Wood is not far from here.'

Galen was sunk in his bitter mood. 'We know where to look. But it's worse than we thought. They may know who they have. If they do, we're finished.'

'They'd have already killed her,' the Sekoi put in.

'Maybe. But even if they have no idea who she is, the child's mind will already be twisted against us. This won't be a simple rescue. She won't want to come. It will be a kidnap.'

Thinking of the girl's spiteful grin, Raffi thought he was more right than he knew.

'And anyway,' he said aloud, 'how do we get in?'

Galen smiled, strangely. 'You know how. Carys must get us in.'

Tallis looked up. 'Who is Carys?'

The Sekoi pulled a face. 'That would take some explaining, Guardian. She's a Watchspy. She may, or she may not, be a friend of ours.'

'Of course she is,' Raffi said hotly. He banged the empty cup down, annoyed. 'She helped me. I saw her.'

'The Makers helped you,' Galen muttered. 'And they appeared in forms your mind would recognize. But certainly Carys is our only way into a Watchhouse, so she must be told.'

The Sekoi looked uneasy, but it said nothing.

Tallis stared into the fire. 'And if she betrays you?'

'She's had that chance before.' Galen glanced at her, his face edged with flame. 'I believe the Makers want her. They are stronger than she is.'

For a moment, in the silence, an owl hooted softly outside. Then Galen tugged a string of the green and black crystals from round his neck and began to wind them absently round his hand, something he only did when he was really troubled. 'There is one thing in the vision that concerns me even more,' he said at last.

The Sekoi edged forward. 'And me.'

Raffi had been dreading this. 'You mean the thing in the Pit.'

'Yes. The thing writing in the dark room.'

They were silent. Even here the mention of the Pits of Maar chilled them. No one had ever gone into them and come back; whatever horrors Kest had begun were still there, in all his workrooms and laboratories, breeding and mutating out of control.

Tallis too, looked grim. She got up and closed the door, and when she came back they saw she was an old woman again, her hands frail. Carefully she lowered herself into a wooden chair. Then she said, 'Tell us what worries you, keeper. All secrets are safe here.'

Galen wrapped the beads around his fingers. Finally he said, 'I've never told anyone this. Ten years ago, when he was dying, my master told me a great mystery. He told me that many who had been high in the Order had suspected something so terrible that they dared not record it; it had never been written down. It was based on an ancient lost text of Tamar's, and on rumour, dark talk, the gabblings of a few, barely sane, who had claimed to have seen it in visions.'

'It?' the Sekoi breathed.

Galen looked away. When he spoke again his voice was harsh. 'The rumours were that Kest had not tampered only with animals. His last experiment, they say, was on a man.'

Raffi stared. He felt the terror of the dream sweeping back over him; for a moment the Pit gaped under him and he felt himself falling into it; snapping his eyes open as the Sekoi hissed.

The room seemed much darker. He was afraid now, wished Galen had never spoken of this. Fighting to stop trembling, he edged closer to the fire.

Tallis said, 'I have never heard this. Could even Kest do something so monstrous?'

Galen took some time to answer. Finally he said, 'Who knows. These are whispers and dreams. But if Kest had meddled, if he had taken a man and made something else out of him, something grotesque, a creature that could live long lifetimes, that had an evil intelligence greater than any animal's, what an enemy that would be.'

'Living in the dark,' the Sekoi muttered. 'Letting others do its work.' The creature's fur was swollen round its neck; it looked tense and distant.

'Your people know about this?' Galen asked.

The Sekoi's yellow eyes blinked. It put its cup down slowly, as if choosing what to say. 'There is a name,' it muttered, 'in the darkest of our stories. A being. Not a man, not Sekoi, not a beast. A creature of evil. Immortal, too hideous to look on. We call it the Margrave.'

The fire cracked, splitting a log in a shower of sparks. The Guardian tapped the chair arm. 'If you feel able, Raffi, can you tell us more about what you saw? Was it a man?'

'I don't know.' He couldn't, he didn't want to think of it clearly; the memory dodged away, was a cold terror. His hands shook and she noticed and put her own over them. 'Don't be afraid, not here.'

He looked up at her. 'I think ... it had been a man. The shape of the face was too long ... I didn't see it properly.'

'If you had you would not be speaking.' She turned to Galen.' 'You think he saw this thing?'

'I think the Makers are warning us,' he said bleakly. 'We've always wondered at the Watch, how it grew so fast, how it defeated us, and all the time none of us knew where it came from. If this is the mind that rules the Watch, then it's still the legacy of Kest ...'

No one answered. Galen rubbed his face wearily.

It was the Sekoi who stirred, kneeling suddenly and piling new logs on the fire, so the dry wood crackled cheerfully. 'None of this concerns us now,' it said firmly. 'We have to find this girl-cub. And I suppose you're right about Carys, keeper, though you know I have doubts about her. How will we send to her? Shall I go?'

Galen glanced up, his eyes black and sharp. 'Thank you, but no. I'll tell her. The Crow will tell her.' Tallis was watching him, intent; he smiled, and at once the sense of weariness among them broke; Raffi almost felt the warmth creep back into the room. Until the keeper said, 'We leave tomorrow.'

The Sekoi looked doubtfully at Raffi. 'Will he be ready?'

'He'll have to be.' Galen turned to Tallis. 'It's been good to live in this place. Even though we have to leave it, it cheers me to know it's still here.'

The Guardian smiled at him. 'For those who hold the Faith, keeper, it will always be here.'

Standing on the wet lawns in the morning, looking back at the house, Raffi knew what she meant. He thought that Artelan's Well had put something in him that hadn't been there before, something so deep he could hardly feel it. But it was there, a small hard gem at the centre of him. He touched it with his sore mind. It was no use wishing they could stay; it would be too hurtful even to think of that.

Before them the wicker walkway stretched into mist; beyond it the Unfinished Lands steamed and hissed. Tallis kissed each one of them and stood back, her arms at her sides.

'May Flain go with you. May Tamar be at your back and Soren smooth your way. And when you find her, bring the child to us. For anything the Watch can do, we can undo.'

Bleakly, Galen nodded. Then he turned, and led them into the fog.

Standing in Line

18

*I saw my brother suffer a hundred years
of remorse.
He had worked with evil and fought to be
free of it.
I saw how despair turned cold in his heart.*
                    Apocalypse of Tamar

Carys stepped between the two oak trunks, warily.

In the deep hollows, crisp leaves were piled; she stood knee-high in the forest's debris. Above, the gnarled branches rustled in every breeze, a new gilt shower tinselling down. Under the slow pattering, she waited.

The wood was silent, its pathways lost behind trunks and branches.

But she knew they were here.

Careless, she leaned back against the oak trunk, squatting down in the fork between immense sprawled roots. Her crossbow was loaded. She could wait.

The dream had come two nights ago, just when she was running out of lies to tell Braylwin. A great black bird had perched on the end of the bed, some village girl's bed she had borrowed for the night, and it had spoken to her with Galen's voice.

'Keilder Forest,' it had said. 'Near the Watch-house.' And then it had gone, flapping out of the window as if it had really been there.

She turned at a cracked twig. A skeat eyed her coldly, then turned and padded off among the

155

bracken. As she watched it, she glimpsed a sharp face looking at her between branches and glanced away to hide a grin. It was the Sekoi.

Galen came out first, brushing between ferns, Raffi a shadow at his back. They squatted.

'Took your time,' she said coolly.

'We had to make sure you were alone.'

'The Watch are never alone.'

'Neither are the Order.' Galen looked sharp, as if power moved in him.

She grinned over his shoulder at Raffi. 'You look older.'

To her surprise that startled him, even scared him. 'Do I?' he breathed.

'Well, don't worry. Not that much.'

The Sekoi had ambled over; it crouched in the deep leaf-drift. 'All together again,' it muttered. 'How cosy.'

She made a face at it.

'We've found the Interrex,' Galen said quickly. 'At least we know where she is.'

'She?'

'We think so.'

'In this forest?'

He looked hard at her, then tipped his head to where the distant edge of the Watchhouse roof showed beyond the trees. 'There.'

Carys stared, astounded. 'In a Watchhouse!'

'We think so,' he said again.

She whistled, then shook her head, pulling a leaf out of her hair absently. 'No wonder you want me! How do you know she's in there?'

'The Makers told us.' He was watching her steadily; she knew he suspected her, that he guessed something. Abruptly, she laughed. 'I never know what you mean when you say that, Galen. Well, if she is in there you've got your work cut out. She'd probably slit your throat rather than let you take her.'

That stung him. His face darkened, and she saw suddenly how he hated this, that even the heir of the Emperors should have been tainted and corrupted by his enemies. And she hated it too. So much, she even surprised herself.

She tucked a stray hair behind one ear. 'So what's the plan?'

'I thought I'd leave that to you. You know these places.'

Indeed she did. Grim, bare classrooms, icy court-yards, the stark dormitories, the punishments, the ones who sobbed in the dark, who disappeared one day, never to be seen again. The guards, the passwords. Nowhere to hide. No way out. And what it did to you.

She looked up at him, suddenly. 'Listen, Galen, get out of here. Go now! Go quickly!'

At once the Sekoi hissed, its yellow eyes nar-rowing, 'What do you mean?'

'She means,' Galen said softly, 'that we're sur-rounded by the Watch.'

The creature leapt up with a snarl. Galen never took his eyes off Carys.

'I can explain,' she muttered.

'I'm sure you can.'

'If you knew, why did you come?'

'Because I wanted to find out why.'

Harness clinked in the wood. Raffi was on his feet, feeling the sense-lines shatter, praying that Galen knew what he was doing.

Ten men on horses faced them. Each crossbow was firmly aimed. The horses were painted red; the men wore the black patrol-helmets of the Watch, their eyes bright in the slits. On the end of the line sat an extraordinary figure; a fat man in a

157

great waxed coat, his puffed face rimmed with black oily hair, perfectly curled. He smiled, his swollen fingers tossing the reins. 'You must introduce me to your friends, sweetie.'

'Drop dead,' Carys muttered. Her face was hot and angry.

Slowly, Galen stood up and turned. He stood, feet apart, staring calmly across the clearing. 'I'm Galen Harn, Relicmaster of the Order of Keepers.'

Braylwin smirked. 'Are you now. And I'm Arno Braylwin, Captain of the Watch, Spymaster, first Grade, Thief-taker, Interrogator of sorcerors.'

Raffi felt cold. He couldn't take his eyes off the nearest crossbow. One twitch, he thought, and sweated with the effort to keep still.

Braylwin gave a haughty nod.

One of his men slid down and brought a small wooden set of steps, garishly painted, which he put in the leaf-drift. One hand on the man's shoulder, Braylwin climbed unsteadily down. Then he flicked some leaves off a log with his coat-tail and sat down.

The Sekoi snarled at Carys. 'You betrayed us,' it hissed. 'I always knew you would.'

'I had no choice!' Suddenly it was all too much. She scorched into temper, leaping up and pushing Raffi aside so fiercely that he lost balance and crashed into the thick drift of leaves. Crossbows swivelled after him. He lay still.

'He knows something about me! I thought it would help if I told him about you, and it was a way of telling you about the Interrex! For Flain's sake, Galen, I never thought you'd really find her!'

The Sekoi spat. 'Playing both sides, as ever.'

Galen stood listening, silent.

Carys marched up to Braylwin and stared down at him, her hand quivering with fury. 'But this slug has brains. He's like a shadow. Whatever I tried I couldn't throw him off.'

She turned her head, suddenly not sure who she was angry with. 'I'm sorry, Galen. All of you.'

'Impressive.' Braylwin looked at her admiringly. 'You'll go far. I almost believe it myself.'

Stubbornly, she glanced at Raffi. He looked away. What was she doing? What was she really up to?

Galen stirred, ignoring the taut bows. He looked coldly down at the Watchlord. 'I'll give you no information, no matter what you do.'

Braylwin shrugged. 'It doesn't matter. The boy will talk.' He smiled, easily. 'Believe me, I know. I've seen them scream and beg to tell me anything, even to die. He looks terrified already.'

Leaves pattered in the bitter silence. Braylwin scratched his cheek with a thumbnail. 'So. The Interrex exists and is in the hands of the Watch! It seems all your dreams are in ruins, keeper. It also poses an interesting little problem for me, actually. After all, I don't want to tell the school-master in there why I want her. There'll be a stiff reward for this one, and I don't intend to share it.' He glanced over. 'Except with my loyal staff, of course.'

Carys glared at him. She looked so cold and expressionless Raffi was suddenly icy with terror – the sense-lines wreathed round the backs of his hands, raising the small hairs.

She raised the crossbow, slowly, until it was poin- ting directly at Braylwin's head.

He smiled, sweating slightly. 'Don't you love your uncle, then, Carys? You ought to, you know. Fire that weapon and you and these will die in the same shower of bolts, and that would be a shame now, wouldn't it. Such a promising career.'

The bow didn't waver. Confused, a few of the horsemen aimed at her, reluctantly.

'He's right.' Galen's voice was harsh and steady. He watched, a half-smile on his hooked face, his eyes dark and sharp. 'It wouldn't be worth it, Carys.'

She whirled so the bow faced him. 'Maybe I should kill you, then. Profitable for me, better for you. Better than torture, anyway. I've seen what they'll do to you.'

Dry-mouthed, Raffi watched. No one was looking at him any more but he didn't dare to crawl away.

'I think,' Galen said softly, 'you should remember your own first rule. Isn't it something about the Watch always being watched?'

He moved, walking slowly towards her while the Sekoi fidgeted with terror. Coming close, he put a hand on the bow and pushed it gently down. Taints of purple sparked from the keeper's fingers; Carys saw them and stared.

The bolt smacked into dry leaves.

At the same time, out of nowhere, arrows slashed across the clearing into the Watchmen, sending their horses swirling in a sudden crashing, whinnying panic. A bolt slammed into a tree above Raffi; he rolled, scrambling and wriggling deep under the leaves and away.

When he raised his head and looked back, Galen and the Sekoi hadn't moved. Neither had Braylwin. But five Watchmen lay still, and the rest were scrambling from their horses' tangled harnesses.

Around them, among the trees, a warband laughed and mocked; a dirty, gold-decked, gaudy army, dressed and painted in crazy colours, their horses' manes tangled with bright ribbons.

Galen looked at Braylwin. 'You may be ruthless, my lord. But here's someone who could give you lessons. I too have my troublesome shadow.'

Braylwin stood and stared at the tiny man in the blue quilted robe who was leaping from his horse.

'You may have heard of him,' Galen said drily. 'His name is Alberic.'

The dwarf grinned, immensely pleased. 'This is a feast, Galen Harn, a feast! Not only you and that tale-spinner, but a Watchlord! A ripe, fat, money-dripping Watchlord!' He was hugging himself in delight, dancing a few happy steps among the leaves. 'Down, boys and girls! Pick up those bows. Whip some rope round our prisoners.'

Appalled, Braylwin glowered. 'You can't. You wouldn't dare . . .'

'Shut it, flesh-pile!' Instantly Alberic's joy died. His shrewd eyes flicked round the clearing. 'Wait!' Then he whirled on Galen and roared the question the keeper had been waiting for.

'Where's your scholar? And where's that girl!'

19

*The stupid must be cast aside. Those of
medium intellect are of most use. Beware
the ones who are too clever. They may be
taught to hate us yet.*

Rule of the Watch

Close up, the Watchhouse was immense, a squat,
ugly building of black brick, dumped in the forest.
All around stood its defences; a fence of spiked
logs, a ditch, and one drawbridge, lowered now,
for the children to straggle across.

From his hiding-place under the thorns, Raffi
watched them forming up in lines, many staggering
under the weight of logs and kindling; even the
smallest children had their arms crammed full.
There were three guards; two laughing and joking
together, the last calling up to someone at a
window. None of them was watching the trees.

Carys nudged him sharply, and was gone.

He hoisted the wood-bundle up against his face
and stumbled out behind her, his heart thudding
like a hammer-bird's knock. The sense-lines
snagged under his eyelid; he knew Alberic's
hunters were only metres behind.

And still he couldn't believe what he was doing.

'Line up!' Someone shoved him; he kept his
head down, praying numbly. Children closed in
behind. Quickly, they began to walk.

The branches were heavy, but they kept him
hidden, and the boy next to him didn't even glance
across. There was no talking, no pushing. In the

silence he could even hear the leaves falling, and the whistle of an oat-piper far off in the wood. Then wooden planks were under his feet; the children's boots rang in hollow echoes. They were crossing the drawbridge.

Glancing up, he saw the archway gaping over him, a great mouth, one lantern hanging from it like a single tooth. This was it. He didn't know any passwords, any rules. Carys would get in but they were bound to find him, drag him out, beat him. He closed his eyes.

She jolted against him. 'Stay close.'

The arch swallowed them. He sensed it over him, felt suddenly small, as if his personality had shrunk, become crushed. Defiantly, miserably, he mumbled the Litany.

The smell of the place was overpowering. Old frowsty rooms, stale fat; a smell of fear, long-enclosed, as if the windows were never opened. And it was bitterly cold.

As the line shuffled on, he glanced at Carys; to his surprise he saw something like hatred on her face. She moved up to him, but before she could speak the line halted.

Ahead the children were chanting numbers to a bored-looking woman on a stool; then one by one they disappeared through a doorway. Nervously, Raffi waited his turn.

'Next,' the woman said, not looking up.

He had decided what to say.

'914,' he stammered, then walked on fast, in case she raised her eyes from the page and looked at him. In seconds Carys was behind him; there was no outcry. It seemed to have worked. In relief he breathed his thanks to Flain.

They found themselves going down a dim stairway; at the bottom was an evil-smelling cellar where the children were stacking the wood. Their silence scared Raffi. They didn't laugh, or joke, or even smile. And he saw how they all watched each other, slyly, as if none of them were friends, or to be trusted.

Carys pulled him gently by the sleeve, then turned and marched out of a different door. Trying to look calm, he followed. She looked as if she knew where she was going. Through a warren of crypts and cellars, up some stairs, then into a corridor where the roof leaked. Opening the first door on the left she peered in, drew her head out, and nodded.

They slid inside, and closed the door tight.

It was a storeroom. Barrels were stacked against a cracked wall. The hearth was a drift of wind-blown ashes.

Raffi breathed out slowly. Then he said, 'I can't believe we're in.'

She went over and knelt on top of the barrels, rubbing dust from one pane of a tiny window. 'Keep your voice down.'

'Will they come in here?'

'It's unlikely.'

He looked at her back. 'How did you know about it? How did you know your way?'

Cold suspicions moved in him like eelworms, but she turned and stared at him contemptuously. 'Don't be stupid, Raffi. These places are all the same – if you know one, you know them all. The Watch pride themselves on that. Wherever you go, always the same. One big family.'

She turned back to the window but he still watched her. Quietly he said, 'So you knew this room somewhere else?'

For a while he thought she wouldn't answer. Then she said, 'It was the one I spent hours in at

Marn Mountain. I had it all worked out. The rotas were easy to alter – everyone thought I was in some other class. I kept food here, books, all the things you weren't allowed. I did it for years, till they found out.'

'What did they do to you?'

'They promoted me, of course.' She turned and grinned at him. 'In the Watch, the slyer you are the better. You look shocked.'

'I just . . .' He shook his head. 'I always assumed you liked it.'

'Liked it!' She spat viciously into the ashes. 'These places are hell, Raffi! You've got no idea. Come up here.'

He climbed up beside her. She rubbed the spot on the window wider, and looking through it he saw a grim courtyard, with a high spiked wall. Children huddled round. Some sat in groups, others ran to keep warm, but there was still little noise, except from one end of the yard where a group silently watched three boys beat a smaller one, punching him in the face and stomach while he sobbed. Raffi stared in horror. 'Why doesn't someone stop them?'

Carys smiled grimly. 'It's probably a punishment. Look.'

Two Watchmen were standing behind the crowd, their arms folded, laughing. One shouted encouragement.

Raffi turned away. He was white with anger. 'No wonder Galen hates the Watch. How can they make the children punish each other?'

'They don't make them. They volunteer.' She climbed down and sat beside him.

'Volunteer!'

'You get better food. And credits on your work-card. The more of those the better you do. I'll bet Braylwin collected plenty.'

'What about you?' He stared at her. 'Did you "volunteer"?'

'Sometimes.' She said it softly, looking away from him. 'They teach you how to use people here, Raffi. I never realized that until after. To hunt and lie and lay traps but never to care. And you have to survive, you have to get through it somehow. Have you ever thought of what happens to those who don't?'

Numb, he shook his head.

'Well, they vanish. It's said they're thrown down the Pits. The Watch has no failures.'

In silence they heard a bell ring, far off in the building. The scuffles stopped outside. Then Raffi said, 'Where do we look for her?'

'We don't, yet. At five bells they all parade in that yard for name-check. Then you'll have to see if she's there. You haven't told me how you know what she's like.'

He shrugged. 'It doesn't matter. Then what?'

'From where she stands in line I'll know where she sleeps. But listen. If I get caught you don't know me. Understand? You just walk by. One of us has to get her out.'

'I can't,' he muttered.

'You can. You'd better. Because if you're caught that's what I'll be doing.'

He didn't know whether to believe her or not.

All afternoon they stayed hidden in the cramped storeroom, except that every hour Carys led him out through a maze of corridors, walking quickly, looking at no one, coming back to the room when the patrol would have looked in and passed on.

'The sweep, we call it. Two men check every

room in the whole house constantly. It took about an hour at Marn. You have to time it just right.'

Bewildered, Raffi sat on the floor. The place upset him. He dared not send out sense-lines, they touched things that made him feel sick. Odd noises and cries echoed in the building; he had glimpses of desolate classrooms, like the one in his vision. He felt trapped, totally cut off. 'And if we find her,' he muttered, 'how do we get her out? Or help Galen?'

Carys licked thirsty lips. 'Galen can take care of himself. But you're right about one thing. Getting in was easy. I haven't a clue how we're going to get out.'

They didn't notice the darkness come. But after a while the room was too dim for them to see each other clearly, and the faintest edge of Agramon was glimmering from somewhere high over the roofs.

A bell rang. Raffi was already sick of them, but Carys stiffened. 'Name-check.' She jumped up on to the barrels. 'Right. Get ready.'

The courtyard was dark now and lit with flares: garish red flames that crackled and guttered in the cold wind, sending shadows leaping. The Watch-children were lining up, silent and sullen, in identical rows rigidly spaced, feet apart, arms behind their backs, eyes fixed on the ground. They wore thin clothes; most were shivering. Raffi ran his eyes anxiously along the lines, past thin boys, tall lanky girls, a sobbing infant everyone ignored.

'Well?'

'I can't . . . yes! That's her! Third from the end, in the back row! That's her!'

Carys pushed him aside and put her eyes to the pane. She saw a small stubborn-looking seven-year-old, her red hair hacked off, her face freckled, already thin. 'Are you sure?'

'Certain. I'd never forget her.'

She spent a long time looking, then turned and leaned back thoughtfully against the wall. She was oddly silent, Raffi thought. A tinge of sadness came out of her and touched his sense-field.

'Right.' She lifted her head firmly. 'We need to plan this. Get her on her own. Diversionary tactics. Something to deal with any pursuit.' She grinned, slyly. 'Just like they taught us.'

He looked baffled.

Carys laughed. 'Don't worry, Raffi. I was always top of the class. Look, that thing you did in Tasceron, the bangs and flashes, the inner eye thing, can you do it here?'

He shrugged, uneasy. He was cold, and hungry, and he loathed this place; the very air was miserable. 'There's no awen here.'

'Awen?'

'Energy, power. Life.'

He shivered, and she felt anxious. 'But you'll do your best?'

'Of course I will. But, Carys, it'll take an army to get us out.'

Angry, she shook her head. 'One step at a time.' Unstrapping her crossbow, she loaded it, then pulled a small pouch from under her coat. Opening it, she took out some fine rope, candles, a tinderbox, some tiny boxes and a package wrapped in black cloth.

He touched the package and she saw his eyes widen. 'This is a relic!'

'Yes.' She shoved it back. 'I got it in the Tower of Song. It's for Galen. Now come on, Raffi. We've got to be ready in an hour. Before the patrol comes round.'

It was exactly an hour and a half later that Carys walked cautiously down the middle of dormitory 27, glancing at the bednumbers, the sleeping huddles under grey blankets. The bed she wanted was third from the end, near where the night-candle spluttered in its lantern. She leant down and took a deep breath. Then, quickly, she twitched the girl over, clamped a cold hand tight on her mouth and hissed, 'Don't scream. Don't speak, just listen.'

Wide brown eyes stared up at her.

'My name is Carys Arrin. I'm a Watchspy, silver rank.' She dangled the insignia carelessly in the child's face. 'You've been selected for a special mission. It's highly secret; none of the other children must know. Do you understand?'

The girl nodded. Her body was tense in the bed.

'You must come with me now. Get dressed, and hurry.'

She took her hand away and stood back. This was the test; if the girl screamed . . . Carys folded her arms and looked away up the room, as if she was impatient. But the child dressed silently, hastily. She was used to obeying orders, as they'd expected, though once or twice she peeped up, curious, into Carys's face.

'Come on!' Carys growled.

'I am!' the girl said impudently. She pulled on her shoes and went back to the bed. Plunging her hand into the straw, she pulled something out and turned, but Carys had seen. 'What's that?'

'Nothing.'

'Liar.' Carys came and snatched it; the girl glared, furious. 'He's mine! And I'm bringing him!' The hiss was loud, but Carys barely heard it. In her hand was a small stuffed toy, a nightcub, so battered one ear was gone, and the dark fur almost rubbed away.

The girl snatched it back, and pushed it into her dress. 'I'm not going without him.'

Carys was amazed. There were no toys allowed in Watchhouses – for the girl to have kept it this long meant she was cunning. Incredibly cunning.

'All right. Follow me.'

She turned and marched down the dormitory, the little girl pattering beside her. In the silence their footsteps sounded loud; Carys felt sweat chill her back. But no one woke.

Once outside she hurried, up the steps, then up again to the dim landing. Lamps burned down long corridors. Far below, the endless patrol closed and opened doors.

'Where are we going?' the girl demanded suddenly.

'Wait and see.' Carys stopped. 'Raffi?'

He stepped out behind them, and the girl stared at him, her brown eyes solemn. 'Who's he?'

'He works with me.'

'I've seen him before. I saw him in a dream.'

Aghast, Carys looked at him. 'What?'

Raffi bit his lip. 'It's all right,' he stammered.

'No it's not. You're from the Evil Order.'

'No . . . Listen.'

But the girl's voice was louder. 'I don't believe you. Where are you taking me?'

Carys clamped her hand tight over the girl's mouth, crouching. 'Keep quiet! I told you, this is a secret!'

The child's eyes blazed; she squirmed with anger, then clenched her teeth on Carys's fingers and bit down, savagely. With a gasp, Carys snatched her hand back.

The little girl looked at Raffi, a cold look.

Then she opened her mouth and screamed.

20

To open and close,
build and destroy,
move forward and back,
to bless and to curse...

Litany of the Makers

'They've done what!'

'Entered the Watchhouse.' Alberic spread his tiny hands to the fire, looking up slyly at the stricken face. 'It's nice to know I inspire such terror. Sit down, Relicmaster, before you crumble.'

Numb, Galen crouched. 'Are you sure?'

'Sikka's group tracked them. Saw them go in – quite cleverly done, they said.' He crooked one finger, and a small table was brought and propped unsteadily on the cave floor. A crystal goblet was placed on it, into which Godric carefully poured an expensive golden cordial. Tied in a damp corner, Braylwin gazed at it enviously. He had already complained so much they had gagged him.

Galen was staring into the flames. Alberic drank daintily, wiped his mouth with his hand and leaned forwards. 'I want to know why. What's in there that's so important? If your boy's caught he'll be skinned alive. I've tracked you this far and all the time I've wondered what you were after.'

Galen stirred, rubbing his chin wearily. His eyes were black, his long hair glossy as a crow's wing. When he looked up there was a tension in his face. 'Do you remember what I once said to you?'

Quizzically Alberic spread his hands. 'Which time?'

'Last time. At the marsh. I told you you've got nothing in your life worth having, despite all your wealth.'

The dwarf grinned, sipping the liquid. 'Oh. That old yarn.'

'No faith. Nothing to fire your soul. You're tired of thieving, war-lord. I can feel it.'

'Indeed.' The tiny man pursed his lips. 'Keeper, are you trying to convert me?'

'I'm trying to save you. Or let you save yourself.'

Alberic winked up at Godric. 'He's appealing to my better nature.'

'You haven't got one, chief.'

'He has,' Galen muttered.

Alberic turned. 'Isn't it nice to know, boys and girls, that our souls are causing such concern! Flain himself couldn't be more worried.'

Giggles echoed round the cave. Galen ignored them, his stare unmoving. 'Under your laughter you're listening, little man.'

'And what must I do, hmm?' Alberic mocked. 'Learn the Book of the Seven Moons by heart? Live on bread and water? Give all my money away to the poor?'

A roar of laughter broke out around him. Into it Galen said quietly. 'None of these. I want you to attack the Watchhouse.'

The Sekoi hissed. Alberic stopped drinking and stared in utter astonishment. The cave was silent.

Finally the dwarf managed to speak. 'What?' he whispered.

'You heard. Raffi and Carys will need to get out. I want you to give them the chance. Give the Watch something to think about. A short attack, then withdraw. None of your people need be hurt.'

Alberic leaned forward, staring at Galen as if he thought the keeper was insane. He seemed too amazed even to laugh. 'And what exactly will you give me for this act of total recklessness?'

Galen shrugged. 'The blue box.'

'The blue box is mine already.' The dwarf pointed to the pack lying dimly in a corner. 'As is that Cat-liar's belt of gold. Have you got anything else that would interest me?'

'One thing.'

Alberic's eyes were greedy. 'What?'

'Your soul.'

The silence was profound. Only the crackle of the fire broke it. And then Alberic bent over, wheezing, and when he straightened they saw he was laughing helplessly, crying with laughter, and all his warband roared with him, the tears rolling down their cheeks, hooting and screaming themselves into an exhaustion of hilarity.

Braylwin giggled too, a dry mockery. The Sekoi closed its yellow eyes and snarled. But Galen never moved, never flinched, watching the dwarf as if he could see right into him, as he gasped and clutched his chest and kicked his legs helplessly against the stool.

Finally, wiping his eyes, Alberic struggled to speak. 'Oh God, you're so good for me, Galen,' he gasped. 'I'm almost tempted to keep you alive. My own tame preacher.' He scratched his cheek and all at once the laughter in his crafty face had gone, and he looked at the keeper hard. 'Tell me what's in that Watchhouse,' he said. 'Tell me. If it's worth getting out I might think about it.'

Slowly, Galen stood up. He turned and looked at Braylwin. The huge Watchman smirked and widened his eyes over the dirty gag. They both knew he dared not tell Alberic about the

Interrex, knew what a prize she would be. Galen frowned, his eyes black. Then he swung to the Sekoi. 'I suppose we'll have to tell him.'

'I suppose so,' the creature said doubtfully. Its fur was lifting with tension; its yellow eyes stared at him. 'He'll want a share.'

'Of course he will. Will there be enough?'

It shrugged, unhappily. 'It means less for the Great Hoard.'

Galen's eyes shifted. Alberic hadn't moved, but he was already more alert, the sense-lines sparking round him.

'So now,' he said softly, 'you're going to pretend this Watchhouse is stuffed with gold?'

Neither of them spoke. Around the cave, talk hushed; most of the warband not guarding the approaches were crammed inside, keeping warm. Suddenly, they were interested.

Reluctantly, the Sekoi stood up, its head bent under the low roof. 'I suppose I'll have to explain.'

'Oh no!' Alberic waved a hand sharply. 'No stories! Not that again. Godric!'

The bearded man was there already; he raised his crossbow lazily and pointed it at the creature with a grin. 'I'm watching you, Greycat.'

The Sekoi made a spiteful, spitting noise.

'Right. Talk.' Alberic leaned back. 'But any hint of a spell and that bolt flies.'

Uneasy, the creature looked sidelong at Galen. Then it spread its seven-fingered hands. 'You have no reason to trust us, thief-lord, I know that. I think the keeper is wrong to tell you this, because how do we know that you won't kill us when you learn it, and take the gold anyway?'

Alberic's shrewd face creased into smiles. He swirled the wine in his cup. 'Go on.'

Galen went and leaned beside Braylwin, half in

shadow. The Sekoi's eyes followed him. 'The keeper leaves me in the dangerous place.'

'Never trust a reckless man,' the dwarf said, drinking.

'I'm beginning to believe you're right.' It stroked its tribemark warily. 'Well, I will tell this plainly. You will have heard, of course, of the Great Hoard . . .'

Alberic was listening now.

'No one but the Sekoi know its purpose. But it is vast, and all our lives we add to it. Last year a tribe near here had all their gold loaded on waggons – ten of them, piled high – and they sent it . . . where we send it. They had to pass through this forest. Normally, we can evade the Watch. However, this time it seems there was some problem.'

'Problem?' Alberic said sweetly.

'They were ambushed. All were killed. The Watch took the gold and have kept it inside the House. Among it were some relics, made of precious metals, which are what the keeper wants.'

'The boy went into a Watchhouse for a few relics?'

The Sekoi looked uncomfortable. It bent forward and said quietly, 'These people are fanatics, my lord.'

'So I've heard.' Alberic folded his hands. 'All this is so interesting! Isn't it interesting, Godric?'

'Thrilling,' the big man muttered, his bow never flinching.

'Ten waggons of gold! Worth doing a lot for. Worth attacking for. More than a small attack, though, wouldn't you say?' He glanced slyly at Galen, who watched darkly. 'More like a small war, that would be. People get killed in such attacks. Children. I never liked children.'

175

Galen glanced at the Sekoi, who shrugged. Alberic wheezed a sudden laugh. 'Oh, don't get too worried, keeper. You don't think I believe this farrago of nonsense, do you?' He leaned back, stretching out his boots and gazing at them critically. 'Not for one second. Cramps your style a bit, creature, doesn't it, my lad's crossbow?'

The Sekoi smiled, sourly.

Suddenly, Galen stalked forward. Pushing the creature aside, he stood in front of Alberic, tall and grim. 'Will you attack?' he asked harshly.

'No.'

Galen nodded. Ignoring the bow, he tugged the awen-beads off and spread them on the sandy floor; seven rings, overlapping.

'What are you doing?' Alberic said, suspiciously.

Galen didn't answer. Instead he stood behind the circles and raised his hands. At once, the cave seemed darker. Talk stopped. The fire cowered down before him.

'Stop it!' Alberic snapped. 'Sit down.'

Galen began to speak. His words were quiet, intense; Maker-words that no one else knew. Around him, in the dark, sudden blue sense-lines uncoiled and crackled. His face was dangerous, edged with anger.

Alberic stood up. 'Kill him,' he hissed.

The bow in Godric's hands burst instantly into flame. He threw it down with a yell.

No one moved.

Galen looked up and pointed at the dwarf. 'Hear me,' he said, the darkness rustling around him, his voice shaking with effort. 'In the name of the Makers, I curse you, thief-lord. I curse you up and down, from side to side, from front to back. I curse you from fingertip to fingertip, head to toe. I curse you today and yesterday and tomorrow.

I curse all you eat, all you drink, all you speak, all you dream.'

White-faced, the dwarf stared up at him. The cave was black, crackling with power. The fire went out, and still Galen snarled the words remorselessly, his finger pointed, sparks leaping about it.

'May your possessions be dust to you. May your body tremble and rot. May your hair turn white and fall . . .'

'No.' Alberic stepped back, holding up his hands. 'No! Wait!'

' . . . May all your friends betray you. May water, fire, earth and air become your foes. May the horrors of Kest worm into you.'

'Galen!' The dwarf seemed to crumple abruptly, his hands trembling. 'Stop it! Not that I believe . . . You can't do this . . .'

Light crackled from the keeper's hand. It roared into the spaces of the cave; blue stinging snaps of light around the tiny man, crawling over his limbs, around his neck, so that he yelled and squirmed and beat them off.

'From this instant you will begin to sicken. Pain will fill you. Your food will choke you. Six weeks of suffering I lay on you, and when you die your soul will scream for eternity in the Pit.'

'*Enough!*' It was a shriek; it broke from Alberic's twisted mouth like a pain, and he held his hands over his head as if the malice of the words battered him. 'Enough. No more!'

There was silence.

The cave was black and smoky, as if something smouldered.

Galen waited. Slowly he lowered his hand.

Trembling, Alberic clawed his way back to the stool and leaned on it in utter silence, everyone's eyes on him. He tried to drink a sip of wine, but the cup shook too violently in his hand.

When he looked up, his face glistened with sweat.

'I don't believe,' he breathed, 'that even you would wish that on me, keeper.'

Galen didn't answer.

'But ... having considered your story ...' He swallowed painfully. 'Having thought about it ...'

'Will you attack?' Galen asked, grim.

Alberic looked at him, furious, white-faced, his hands still shaking.

'Yes,' he spat.

21

In the unlikely event that all training fails, the agent must use whatever strategies are left.

Rule of the Watch

Instantly a bell began to clang, hard and insistent, appallingly loud. Doors banged open; someone shouted.

Carys cursed bitterly; she grabbed the little girl's arm and twisted it up behind her back with a savage jerk. 'One more sound and I'll break it!' she hissed.

White-faced, the girl stared up at her, pain forcing tears into her eyes. Raffi looked round in terror. 'Come on!' he muttered.

They ran down the corridor, through the lamp-shadows. Turning the corner, they saw two men; instantly Carys pushed the girl aside, raised her bow and fired. One man collapsed, clutching his arm, the other fired back, the bolt embedding in the lintel over Raffi's head. Rolling, Raffi gathered up all his energy and flung it in a flaring explosion down the corridor. There was a bang, and a crackle of light. When the smoke cleared he saw both men were down.

'Brilliant!' Carys hauled the child up and jammed a new bolt in the bow. Raffi ran down to the men and knelt by them anxiously.

'Are they dead?' she muttered.

He looked up, sharply. 'Of course not!'

'Then come on!' As she tugged her away, the

little girl stared back. 'What did he do? What was that?'

'That was the Order at work.' Carys laughed sourly. 'You'd better forget all that stuff they taught you about illusions. These people know a few tricks.'

They ran up the stairs, round a corner, then crouched, breathing hard. Far off the Watchhouse was astir – voices were yelling orders.

'How long?' Raffi muttered.

'They'll check the dormitories. They probably already know she's missing.' Wrathfully, Carys glared down. 'Why couldn't you have kept quiet! And why didn't you tell me about this dream, Raffi?'

He frowned. 'I didn't realize she would ... It was more like a vision. Anyway, it means she really is the Interrex.'

'The what?' the girl asked.

'Nothing.'

Silent, the child surveyed them, especially Raffi. 'In my dream,' she said, remembering, 'you were in the classroom.'

He crouched beside her. 'That's twice you've got me into trouble.'

Her quick face grinned. 'Yes. I'm good at that.'

'I'll bet you are,' Carys said sourly.

'They'll never let you out.' Calmly, the girl pulled the nightcub out and smoothed its head. 'You'll be killed. I won't care.'

Chilled, Raffi reached out and held her thin wrist. 'What's your name?' he asked.

She looked surprised. 'Felnia. What's yours?'

'Raffi.' He turned the insignia on her neck. The number was 914.

They were silent a moment. Impatient, Carys shuffled down to peer round the stairs. 'It's late. I knew that fuse was – ' Before she'd finished, a vast explosion deafened them, shaking the walls; then another, far off in the depths. 'Now!' Carys breathed. Slipping out, she raced ahead, checking every corner, Raffi pulling the little girl hurriedly after. Halfway round the next bend a small cold hand slipped into his. He held it tight.

But there were too many patrols, too many people. Twice they were nearly caught; at last they stumbled into an empty classroom as a group of tall women stalked by, banging open every door and looking in.

Crouched under a desk, Raffi waited for the footsteps to fade. 'What now?' he whispered.

Carys pushed back her hair. 'The front gate is impossible. We won't even get near it.' She scowled. 'Mind you, I never thought we would.'

'Is there any other way out?'

'Not from here.'

'So what do we do?'

'Withdraw. Somewhere we can defend ourselves.' She turned to Felnia. 'The north tower. What do they use that for?'

The girl put her tongue out. Carys shrugged. 'We'll try it. It's usually staff quarters – they may not think we'll go there.'

They moved quickly, putting out every lamp they passed. Then Carys stopped, so abruptly that Raffi ran into her. 'Listen.'

'What?' But as he said it his sense-lines swirled; he felt it intensely in a shiver of sweat, a black, swollen thing, some grotesque six-footed beast slavering down the corridors.

'The bloodhound.' Carys sounded furious. 'We've no chance.' She rammed the bolt home and turned to face the dark.

'Not here!' He grabbed her. 'Up in this tower. We can wedge the doors. Don't give up, Carys!'

She looked at him strangely; he pulled her away. Round the next bend was a door they tugged open, but inside there was no way to lock it, so they raced and gasped breathlessly up the wooden stairs, pushing the girl in front of them. Up a high flight was a kitchen, full of barrels and stores. Carys flung down the bow and grabbed the nearest cask. 'Push them down!'

Gasping with the weight, they toppled the cask and rolled it to the stairtop and over; it crashed down, splintering with an enormous thud against the door below.

'All of them!'

Barrel after barrel they rolled, Felnia pushing with them, all suddenly helpless with giggles, laughing stupidly, as if it was a game, till the stairwell was jammed with splintered wood and sour wine, the reek of cheeses and dried salted fish.

Below, the door jerked, rammed hard, but the barrels clogged it, kept it closed. Someone yelled furious orders.

Carys stopped laughing, clutching her side. 'They'll get an axe. Come on.'

They burst into the top room. Two beds, the blankets sprawled, a chest, a small table. Nothing else. Raffi ran to the window, tugging it open. Then he stood still. Directly below was the ditch, yawning, rammed with sharp, upright spikes.

All at once, cold hopelessness came over him. He felt sick and tired, as if all the energy had gone out of him with that bolt of light. And he knew what Carys had known since the girl screamed. They were finished. There was no way out.

Carys had jammed the table against the door.

Now she sat against the wall, tense, the crossbow aimed.

In the silence he said, 'We can't just wait for them!'

'What else can we do, Raffi?' Wearily she shook her brown hair. 'Never get into a one-way trap, old Jellie used to say. He never said there was sometimes no choice.'

Something clanged below.

Felnia stood by the door, the nightcub still under one arm. Looking at them, she sat cross-legged on the floor and said, 'You could give yourselves up.'

Carys snorted.

'No.' The girl nodded. 'I suppose not.' Her brown eyes fixed on Raffi. 'Why did you want me? Where were you taking me?'

'Out of here.' Suddenly he knelt up close to her. 'We're your friends. We came to rescue you. We were taking you to a place, a beautiful place, full of trees and flowers, peaceful, even in winter. The Watch never come there. Everything you want is there, food and clothes and people to look after you and love you. Wouldn't you like that? Wouldn't you?'

Expressionless, she stared at him. 'No punishments?'

'None.'

'I don't know.' She glanced at Carys. 'Would I like it?'

'Not at first,' Carys said quietly. 'But I think you'd come to like it.'

'Have you been there?'

She looked at Raffi. 'No. But I believe it would be a good place.'

'But why me? Why not Helis, or Dorca?'

'Because you – ' But Raffi stopped, warily. Carys

had given a quick shake of her head; the little girl saw it.

'I won't tell,' she said at once.

Raffi felt a sudden surge of bitterness. Somehow it hurt most that the Interrex might die without even knowing who she was. He knew well enough that when the Watch stormed the room, none of them were likely to survive. 'Do you remember anything, before you came here?'

The girl looked surprised. 'Of course I do. I remember an old woman called Marta. She cried a lot. She gave me Cub.' She frowned. 'Was that my mother?'

Raffi sighed. 'No.'

'Is my mother in this garden you were talking about?'

He glanced despairingly at Carys. 'No. Not your mother.'

The girl nodded. She seemed quite satisfied.

'It's a pity we won't be able to go there,' she said.

Raffi rubbed his hair. He was so terrified he felt like hugging himself tight. 'I wish Galen was here.'

'He'd only end up dying with us.' Carys was listening calmly; now he could hear it too, the regular, harsh thwack of the axe on the distant door.

'Couldn't you lie to them?' he said abruptly. 'Take me prisoner. Say – '

'Raffi.' She looked at him in amusement. 'In this situation I'd have no chance. They'll shoot first.'

'You could call down.'

'I could. Then we'll both be tortured and they'll know all about Tasceron, and the Crow, and the Interrex, and anything else that's in your mind.'

He felt foolish.

She looked back at the door. 'It's strange,' she

said, 'but I always had an idea it would be my own people who would get me.'

'They're not your people,' he said quietly.

The axe splintered through the wood. Warily, Raffi sent a sense-line down to it; he could feel a crowd of Watchmen. At least fifteen. All armed.

But there was something else, too. Faintly, beyond them, beyond the walls of the house, he sensed it. Without knowing, he raised his head, sharply.

Carys glanced over, alert. 'What is it?'

Rippling out, he touched them. Wild people, smelling of the forest. Bright with stolen gold. An army of them.

'Alberic?'

'What?'

'*Alberic*!' He scrambled to the window. 'Look!'

A shower of arrows was slashing over the fences. Men were running; a few fell. Already the draw-bridge was smouldering; as he watched, a blast of familiar white fire shot out of the forest again, roaring the wood into flame. 'That's the box! What's he doing?'

Carys gave a yell of joy. 'It's Galen! He's got them to come!'

'But how?'

'Who cares!'

The axe-thumps stopped. Then, furiously, they came again, faster. Raffi wrenched the window open. A sudden wild idea had come to him, as if it had shot out of the forest like an arrow, and he had caught it. He turned to her. 'Give me that relic!'

'What?'

'The relic!'

She reached into the pouch and threw it. Raffi tore off the black cloth and saw a small grey console, faintly glowing. Holding it tight, he reached into it, felt the Maker-power there, drew it out in long blue lines, sending them spinning down out of the window, long ropes of power, weaving and twisting them into a net, suspended above the deadly spikes.

Below, the door crashed down.

He grabbed the Interrex and forced her up on to the sill. 'Jump! You'll be all right. Quickly!'

Footsteps came warily up the stairs.

'I'll be killed!' She looked down at the spikes, and grabbed him with both hands.

'You won't!'

'I will!'

'For Flain's sake, go!' Carys screamed. 'They're here!'

The door burst open. Instantly she fired. Snatching up the girl, Raffi squeezed himself through the window.

Then he jumped.

The Falls of Keilder

22

*From a high place, Soren looked out at
the Unfinished Lands. 'The winters will
be long now,' she murmured.*
          Book of the Seven Moons

They crashed into the net.

It dipped and sank and steadied, the blue lines
sparking under his hands. He tried to get up and
couldn't; suddenly he felt utterly spent, clutching
the relic tight in case it fell.

Someone was shouting at him and tugging his
hair, then the net plunged again and flung him
over. He moaned, opened his eyes and saw just
below a terrifying glimpse of the sharp stakes.
Then Carys with her shoulder soaked in blood was
hauling at his arm.

'Raffi!' she yelled. 'Come on!'

He staggered over the edge of the net and collapsed on to his knees. The forest seemed a
hundred miles away.

Arrows slashed the air around him. He felt
exhausted, wished they'd leave him alone, let him
sleep, let him crumple, but Carys hauled him up
with one arm under his, calling him vicious names,
and on the other side two small cold hands clasped
tight round his waist.

Half-dragged, he stumbled away from the
Watchhouse, into darkness, into a roar of voices
and one strong grip that heaved him up, over its
shoulder, and away.

When he opened his eyes it was dark, and warm. For a moment he thought he was back in Sarres, but above him was the roof of a cave, seamed with glittering quartz, red in the low glow of a fire. The rocks around him felt calm and ancient. Briefly, deep within them he touched a song, a drift of music so old it barely existed. Then, gradually, memory crept over him, and an ache in his chest that made him catch his breath.

He sat up.

A tiny lamp burned on the sandy floor. Outside, someone was yelling in anger. Alarmed, Raffi pushed the blankets away wearily and stumbled out, but a long hand caught him and steadied him. 'Take care, small keeper!' The Sekoi stood, its sharp eyes bright in the moonlight. 'How do you feel?'

'Terrible. What's wrong with me?'

It shrugged. 'Nothing I can understand. Your master says you did too much in making that magic net.' It winked at him. 'He won't say it, but he's proud of you.'

'Galen!' Weakly, Raffi laughed. He found that very funny.

The Sekoi scratched its fur, and bit a nail. 'You Starmen,' it muttered. 'We'll never understand you.'

It was Alberic who was angry. From the cave-mouth Raffi could see him now, furiously slamming his hands against a tree.

'What's going on?'

'Come and see.' The Sekoi led him outside; he saw Galen standing tall and grim in the dark clearing, arms folded. The keeper glanced across but his face didn't change. Between them Alberic raged, kicking over a stool in uncontrollable fury.

The change in the dwarf astonished Raffi. He

looked pinched and grey; his hair seemed thinner, and his temper was foul. A tipped goblet of wine spilled among the leaves; as they watched, he picked up a gold plate full of fruit and hurled it hard at the bushes with a scream. The Sekoi looked after it, eagerly.

'Are we his prisoners?' Raffi asked, bewildered.

'I think not. Galen has put some fearsome curse on him. In fact, I rather think he's our prisoner.' It slid into the undergrowth, quickly.

Suddenly Alberic stopped raging, breathless. Clutching his side, he swung round. 'You promised me!'

'I promised you nothing.' Galen was remorseless. 'I asked you to attack.'

'We attacked! We burned the drawbridge! Three of my boys are having bolts picked out of them! I even used up all that damnable blue box. What more do you want? Take the stinking curse off me!'

'Not just yet,' Galen said calmly.

Alberic clutched his arms about him like a man in a nightmare. 'For Flain's sake, keeper! Everything I eat tastes like ash!'

'First,' Galen went on, 'you get us out of the forest. We'll need horses – the boy's too worn out to walk. And you protect us from any Watch patrols till we get to the marsh. A day's journey, no more.'

'The marsh?' Despite his pain, Alberic's eyes went sly. 'What's in that marsh?'

'Nothing you'll ever find.' Galen shifted the weight from his stiff leg; he looked grim but Raffi could tell he was enjoying this. 'Agreed?'

The dwarf swore. 'I've no choice.'

'No, you haven't. And if anything happens to

me the curse will never be lifted. Take care of me, thief-lord. Without me six weeks of suffering ...'

'I know! Don't start that again!'

Galen grinned darkly. 'And if my friends are hurt I'd see them die before I'd cure you. Believe me.'

'I'd believe anything of you.' Alberic spat, and watched him sidelong, a murderous look that chilled Raffi. 'But what I really want to know is, did I have to suffer all this just to rescue *that*?'

He jabbed his finger out. Raffi looked over.

Felnia was sitting near a campfire, eating a huge slice of melon; there were pips all over her face. She rubbed them off, fascinated, her brown eyes staring at the dwarf.

'Is he crazy?' she asked.

Galen grinned. 'I hope not. I can't cure that.'

Someone came up behind Raffi. 'Feeling better?' It was Carys. She had a different shirt on, and a bloody slash down her jacket sleeve.

'A bit. What happened to you?'

She frowned, shaking her head. Reluctantly she said, 'I couldn't jump.'

'Couldn't?'

'Too scared.'

He laughed but she looked up quickly. 'I mean it. I saw how it held you, but ... it was only made of light, Raffi!'

He nodded. 'But you did it. Galen would say that was a leap of faith.'

They watched Felnia. She stood up and came out into the dim clearing, deep in leaves. First she looked at Galen, then Raffi. 'Are we going to the garden now?'

He nodded, feeling suddenly happier. Lightning glimmered silently, high above the trees; the girl looked up at it, surprised. 'Good.'

'You're willing to come with us?' Galen asked, harshly.

She pointed. 'With him. I'll go with him.'

Raffi felt foolishly pleased. Then he realized she was pointing behind him, and turned. The Sekoi lurked there, astonished.

'Me?'

'I like you.' The girl took another bite of her melon. 'You're furry,' she said, indistinctly, 'like Cub.'

'Thank you.' The creature looked dubiously at the motheaten toy; moving forward it thrust something from behind its back into Carys's hands. She hid it expertly but not before Raffi had glimpsed the golden plate.

'This is so sickening,' Alberic spat.

The Sekoi crouched on its long knees and held out a seven-fingered hand. 'Shall we go into the cave?' it said quietly. 'Because I think it's going to rain.'

The little girl nodded. As she passed Alberic, she whispered loudly, 'He *is* crazy.'

'Indeed?' the Sekoi said mildly. 'Then that makes two of us.'

That night, in the back of the stuffy cave with the rain crashing outside, the four of them sat on their own, deep among stalactites, with the Interrex asleep in blankets on the Sekoi's lap.

It pulled dirt from her hair, thoughtfully. 'She'll be a handful. She's as haughty as an Emperor's child ought to be.'

Raffi grinned, feeling warm and rested. He'd had plenty to eat, and Alberic's guards prowled the woods for miles around. The Interrex was safe, and they were going back to Sarres, and Braylwin was tied up and guarded somewhere. And yet, he thought sleepily, they were still in the middle of their enemies.

Carys was telling Galen about the Watchhouse. He nodded, grimly. 'It sounds worse than even I thought. You think the child will be satisfied to stay with us?'

'If she's got any sense.'

'What about you?' Raffi said suddenly. 'You can't go back now.'

She shrugged, uneasy. 'Of course I can. No one knows it was me in there.'

'Except Braylwin.' Raffi stopped. Galen's warning had snagged every sense-line he had; he looked down, giddy.

'There's time to decide. It will take a day to ride clear of the forest.' Galen tugged the hair carelessly from his face and knotted it in the dirty string. 'Now one of us stays awake, all night. But first it's time for the Litany, boy. And don't fall asleep.'

It was strange being on a horse again. He and Carys rode together, with the Sekoi and the little girl on a white horse in front of them. Even Galen rode, a green-painted creature with sidelong frightened eyes. They travelled quickly, in the long straggle of the thief-band. The remaining Watchguards, Braylwin's men, had vanished; Raffi didn't know if their throats had been cut or if they'd been released. Certainly Alberic wouldn't have got any ransom for them.

But Braylwin was still there. They'd made him walk at first, but he'd been so clumsy and complained so loudly they'd found a horse for him too, a great stubborn pack-beast. Raffi stared at the man, repelled by his great bulk. As if he sensed it, the spymaster turned round in the saddle and smiled greasily.

'Fond of the lad, aren't you, Carys?'

'Ignore him,' Carys muttered.

But Braylwin slowed his horse, hanging back. 'Won't you release your uncle, sweetheart?' he whispered. 'It would be wise.'

She stared out into the trees, icily.

Braylwin scratched his cheek with plump, tied hands. 'You see, I was just composing my report. What an epic that's going to be! It's a pity you'll never have the chance to read it.'

'What are you going to say about her?' Raffi was worried.

The big man jolted in his saddle and smiled. 'Why, everything I should. Betrayal of the Watch, that's a hanging offence. Abduction. Counter-espionage. Of course, if either of you should decide to help me escape, that would be different. Very different. You and I could make up some really tasty little story . . .'

'As far as I'm concerned you can rot!' she snapped, turning savagely.

'But I won't rot.' The black eyes were sharp in his flabby face. 'I'm rich, Carys,' he hissed, 'and the dwarf's greedy. I can buy freedom. When I do, believe me, I'll have your name on every hanging-list from here to Maar. So hurry up and decide!'

But she urged the horse on, past him, and for a long time after, even when Raffi spoke to her, she wouldn't say a word.

The wood was a morass, and the gale had brought all the leaves down. In the afternoon, drizzle began again; every rider became a grey shape, slithering and splashing through mud and over slippery rutted tracks. As he jolted, Raffi let his third eye open and looked out into the wood, feeling it cower under the leaden weather, the grey dragging rain, all the bare thorns scattering great drops down on his face. Soon he was soaked, holding loosely to Carys's coat, and far off in his dream-sight watched a skeat-pack splash through a swollen stream, tiny larvae scattering between their paws.

The world was dissolving; he felt the whole hemisphere reeling into winter, the long, bitter Anaran winter of ice-storms and raw gales, each year worse than the last; the time when the grass froze and the carnage-wolves prowled down from the Unfinished Lands, when the seven moons glinted frost-bright among the Maker-stars. He shivered. Last year he and Galen had barely come through it. But this year things would be better; they would be in Sarres. If only Galen would stay there.

Darkness came early, a dank autumn twilight, a rain-gloom gathering between the wet twisted boles of the trees. Boulders and great shattered cliffs of dark rock rose about them. Flittermice came out; owls began to hoot from the high caves far above. The Sekoi looked up and listened to them, holding Felnia carefully.

Late in the evening they stopped briefly to eat, but lit no fires; Alberic was determined to press on. He had given up riding; four of his toughest men carried him now in a litter that was gaudily painted and hung with sodden crimson cloth. Godric took him some food but ducked away quickly, the plate flung furiously at his head. Some of the warband laughed; others looked evilly at Galen. Raffi felt afraid.

In the dismal rain it was difficult to see; he sheltered under a larch tree eating bread miserably, water dripping from his hair and fingers. Suddenly everything seemed wrong: Sarres a hundred miles away, his senses dulled and shivering, all the power-lines drawn into the earth like a snail draws into its shell.

Then Galen came up and grabbed him. 'Where is she? Is she with you?'

Bewildered, Raffi stared. 'Carys?'

'Felnia!' Galen's hawk-face was anxious, his hair plastered to his forehead. 'Have you seen her?'

A rainsquall gusted into their eyes. Among the trees, Carys yelled; Galen raced towards her, crashing through the decaying bracken and fat stumps of puffballs, shoving through an interested crowd of the thiefband. Raffi ran after him, dropping the bread.

The Sekoi lay on its back, eyes wide open, staring sightlessly up. Godric was feeling its limbs over carefully. 'Not dead. Some sort of blow to the head.'

Galen whirled round. 'She must have run off!'

'No.' Carys stood stock still. She was staring at something dim in the rainy wood; Braylwin's great packhorse, cropping lichen from a dead log. Sliced rope hung from its neck.

'Oh God, Galen,' she breathed. 'He's got her.'

23

Bind a bright web about the doubtful soul.
If you pull hard, it will come to you.
Apocalypse of Tamar

'And why should I?' Alberic was peevish; he shivered in his quilted robe, a fur-lined cloak clutched tight around him.

'Because if you don't,' Galen stormed, 'I'll go alone and you can burn in your own hell!' The keeper was reckless with black fury; Raffi knew that in this mood he might do anything.

Alberic knew it too.

'All right.' The thief-lord waved a sickly hand. 'Get the lads out, Taran. Search groups of ten. We want the child alive.' He looked at Galen slyly. 'And the fat man? He's good for a thousand marks.'

'I don't care.' The keeper snatched his staff down from the horse, the rain lashing between them. 'Raffi, come with me.' He glanced at Carys. 'You too, if you want.'

She nodded, loading the bow. Her face was taut and white. Raffi felt strange memories in her, and anger. Deep anger.

They slipped between the trees. Galen had his own way of tracking; he followed the glints and taints of feelings, the tiny intricate sense-traces. He led them down a gloomy trail between holly and larch, the trees thickening as they went, the ravine's shattered cliff looming somewhere behind the rain.

Shouts rang in the wood. Behind them Alberic came, scowling and limping, Godric a big shadow behind him.

Galen questioned trees and owls, swiftly, silently, bursting straight to their deep consciousness, leaving them dizzy. He was ruthless, and Raffi felt the sore echoes of it. But Braylwin had come this way. Pictures of them flickered in his third eye: the big man carrying the child easily, under his arm.

'I'm surprised he could go this fast,' he gasped.

Carys glanced back. 'He's fitter than you'd think. He can run when he wants to. All that puffing is an act.'

The trail scrambled down, broke into scree and falling rock. It was dark down here, softened with mist, every branch black and dripping. A were-bird screeched, and Galen slipped, jamming his stick into the mud with a curse.

At the bottom, distorted rowans sprouted, their thin boles white and spindly. The track split in two. Galen crouched, hands on the wet rocks, sending his mind far into soil and puddles and clotted leaves. But Carys darted forward and picked something out of the lefthand track. 'Don't bother. She's Watchtrained, remember?'

It was the toy nightcub. She threw it to Raffi who jammed it in his pocket; Galen was already gone, pushing his way among the sprawling branches. Moss and lichen coated everything; down here the rocks and trees were green in the gloom. It all smelt rich and rotten, the path choked with strange ghostly moonflowers that grew too high, grotesquely twisting after the light.

Crashing through them, Raffi heard water; the roar of it, falling from some unguessed height. Then his sense-lines touched it, and were swept away into a moving flow of energy, patterned by rainbows.

'He's close!' Galen yelled. 'Get ready!'

They burst out into a clearing; before them the black waters of a torrent glinted over the stones. Down the cliff a great waterfall roared, a deafening crash of water, the foam at its base endlessly breaking and whirling away in bubbled white patches.

It was almost too loud to think; the sense-lines jangled, and Raffi felt suddenly dizzy, as if someone had slapped him hard on the side of the head. Galen looked round too, disoriented. 'Can you see him?'

A crossbow bolt thumped into wood behind them; Carys yanked Raffi down instantly among the moonflowers.

'Idiot!' she yelled above the water-crash. 'Keep down!'

At least now they knew Braylwin was armed. And just then, as if the Makers had ordered it, the river mist thinned, and through its frail wisps the seven moons shone clear, a ragged formation that was almost the Arch, though Lar was just a crescent and the strange pitted surface of Karnos was too far down among the trees.

Galen glanced up. He said nothing aloud, but Raffi sensed his prayer, some deep affirmation he couldn't recognize.

'Can you see him?' Carys called.

Galen shook his head. But his eyes were closed; he was feeling with his mind, and on the ground he had laid one ring of awen-beads and a small hazel twig. He turned it in his fingers as they watched, gently.

Then it stopped, pointing across the river, to the right of the falls. Raffi strained his eyes to see what was there, but the dapples of moonlight and the energy-field of the water were bewildering. Stripes of pearl and rose filtered down the rockface.

Galen tugged on the beads. Pulling Carys closer, he said in her ear, 'I'll get him to concentrate on me. You move up the bank.' She nodded; his hand tightened. 'Keep the Interrex safe, Carys.'

She laughed, and said something Raffi couldn't hear; then she was gone, slithering into the moon-flowers. 'Go with her,' Galen yelled.

Raffi hesitated.

'Do as you're told, boy!'

He turned, pushing between the tall stalks, uneasy. Galen was too exposed. The sense-lines were useless here. Everything echoed and rang. He wondered if Braylwin had known this would happen.

Worming along in the moonflowers, he worried about blue spiders and vesps. This was just the sort of place for them, and he'd never even feel them on him. He shivered. Ahead, Carys crawled, and the moons' light quivered on the crashing water.

Then, just below the fall, a flicker of movement over the river caught his eye. He stopped, straining to see in the dimness. From rock to rock near the cliff base a black figure climbed, bulky but swift.

'Carys!' he hissed, but she was too far ahead to hear.

Turning back, Raffi saw Braylwin wedge himself securely, bracing his feet. Then he whipped the crossbow up and aimed it, his eye looking down the bolt. Raffi leapt up, glancing back. Galen stood between two trees, the moonlight catching his shape.

'*Galen!*' Raffi screamed.

The bolt flashed, the keeper turned, and instantly a small figure leapt up at him and tore him down into a crash of shadows. Oblivious of danger, Raffi raced back, flinging himself down breathlessly as Godric came lumbering up.

Both of them stared.

Alberic was sitting up, swearing savagely, picking clots of mud off his cloak, Galen half-lying in the leaves, staring at him. Just above their heads the crossbow bolt had splintered the rowan trunk in half.

'For Flain's sake, you stupid, reckless fool, keep your head down!' the dwarf snarled.

Godric snorted with laughter; his chief glared up at him wrathfully. 'You! Brainless! You're assigned to him. If he dies I'll have you skinned an inch at a time and hung out of my towertop for the crows to pick at! Understand?'

The bearded man nodded, his grin still wide. Galen picked himself up, stiffly. 'You're a better man than you want to be, thief-lord.'

Alberic ignored that. 'A keeper for the keeper,' he said sourly. 'But when this curse is off, Galen, I'll make up for lost time, believe me!'

A shout made them scramble hastily to the river. Looking out, Raffi saw Carys, far off near the falls; she yelled again, pointing.

Braylwin had the girl with him now. In the moonlight they could see how he pushed her ahead of him up the cliff, climbing behind like a vast shadow, and far above in the mist strange birds called, their cries disturbed and wary.

Galen cursed; then he was gone, Godric swiftly behind him. Ignoring the dwarf, Raffi ran after them. They raced along the narrow path, the torrent churning below them. There were huge rounded boulders in the stream; looking up, Raffi saw Carys leaping from one to another, perilously balanced, the waterfall crashing over her.

Braylwin was higher now, the little girl kicking and struggling, sending trickles of stone that rattled down the cliff. The Watchman struck her hard with his fist, but still she fought. Behind them, Carys fired her bow, but deep rocks and springing trees hid them. Shouldering the weapon, she began to climb.

Galen scrambled down to the rocks, crossing recklessly, and Raffi came after him. The roar and speed of the water filled him with fear; one slip and he knew it would whirl him away, crashing him downstream, snapping his limbs against boulders and tree stumps. Cold spray soaked him; his feet slithered every way, he wobbled and leapt through rainbows and the moon-splashed crash of the fall that fell on him heavy as wet snow from a roof. One more jump. He landed on hands and knees in the mud, scrambled up, exhausted.

'*Braylwin!*'

Carys's yell stopped them all.

Slowly, the Watchman turned, crossbow ready.

She was just below him, feet braced, bolt aimed.

'Let her go!' she yelled.

In the moonlight they saw the big man's sour smile. 'You should come with me, Carys. We can share the profits.'

'I'd rather kill you,' she snarled.

He shook his head, the drops of water falling like silver slashes. 'That's better. For a while I thought they'd made a keeper of you. But revenge, that's a Watchman's act.'

'Yes,' she yelled. The bow didn't waver. 'Yes, it is. And this isn't about Emperors or their heirs. This is about me. I don't know who I am, Braylwin. I'll probably never know. All I've learned is hunting and lying, that's all you and your Watchlords want from me, that and never asking any questions. But I don't believe it any more, I've finished with them and you and your lies, because every time I look at that girl I see myself, and all the things you've done to me.'

He laughed, one hand tight on the bow. 'Poor dear Carys. It's hardly my fault.'

'And not just me. All the others too.'

'The whole world, Carys! For the whole world is the Watch now. You'll never get away from it. It's even in you. Deep in you. And it always will be!' He twisted suddenly, grabbed Felnia and thrust her in front of him. Carys didn't move.

'Don't,' Galen said softly, just behind her. 'He's not worth your soul.'

She flicked a glance at him, amused. 'Always trying, Galen. I'll give you that.'

A rock shifted, crashed down. Instantly the little girl screeched and bit; he jerked her away and dropped the crossbow and she jumped, ledge to ledge, like a cat.

The bow clattered endlessly down, then splashed.

Braylwin was alone.

He drew himself up, held his arms wide. 'Well, Carys,' he roared over the falls. 'I'm ready now!'

Carys was still.

'You haven't gone soft on me, have you, sweetie? You know what to do. You have to kill me now, Carys. Or you're finished with the Watch.'

'No!' Galen hissed. 'Carys, listen to me . . .'

'And you want to, don't you!' Braylwin folded his arms. 'Remember your training. Fast and firm. Do it now, girl.'

'Carys. For Flain's sake . . .'

'Shut up, Galen.' Her face was wet. She didn't even look down.

'It's not the way!'

'Of course it is,' she snarled.

Then she fired.

24

*Kest raised himself in great pain. 'I have
done evil and I know it. I went to war
on my own creatures; the dragon is
destroyed but I have to follow it, even to
the caves of death.' He closed his eyes,
Tamar lifting him. He spoke only once
more. 'Beware the Margrave,' he
whispered.*

Book of the Seven Moons

'My ransom!' Alberic's howl rang over the waterfall. 'God rot you, girl, my ransom!'

Galen leapt fiercely up the cliff; he grabbed the
Interrex and swung her down into Godric's grip.
Then he stared up.

'You'll have your ransom, thief-lord.'

Braylwin was standing stock still, his face white.
The bolt had split the rock inches from his left eye.
He reached up and touched it, unbelieving. When
he spoke his voice was only a whisper in the water-
crash. 'So we've lost you, Carys. We've lost you.'

She stood silent, looking up at him. Then she
turned and climbed down, past Raffi, into the
wood.

It took some time to get Braylwin down and
back over the river, Alberic fussing and moaning
the whole while, cursing Galen and the clumsy
bearers. In the end, Godric had to carry him back,
and all the way the thief-girl, Sikka, mocked him
about how much care he was beginning to take of
his enemies.

Raffi was shocked, as if some bolt had gone through him too. He had sensed nothing as Carys had passed him; worse than nothing. An emptiness, black and deep and cold. Stumbling on the path, he shuddered. Had she meant to miss? he thought. Or to kill?

All evening, in the hasty camp they made under the rocks, he waited for her to come back. Completely unworried, Felnia had taken Cub back from him and gone to sit by the Sekoi; it had told her intricate rambling stories until she slept and now it lay, long legs stretched next to the fire, brooding on the pain in its head. Galen was nowhere to be seen, and Alberic was yelling at the grumbling, half-drunken man he called his 'surgeon'.

Raffi moved uneasily. When he looked up, the Sekoi was watching him, its yellow eyes narrowed to slits.

'Why don't you go and look for her?' it said quietly.

He shrugged. 'Do you think I should?'

'I do, small keeper.' The Sekoi chewed a nail thoughtfully. 'Someone should. It would be best if it were you.'

Abruptly, Raffi stood up. He went straight past the sentries and walked back along the river trail, moving quietly in the dark till the noise and stir of the camp were distant.

The forest rustled. Far off, the great falls roared. Sending out sense-lines he touched sleeping trees, their deep consciousness stirring; startled the tiny minds of voles and shrews; woke a weasel that curled back up into weariness.

Then he winced. Something else was there, so sharp it stung him like a black bee. He pushed off the path, through a thick stand of larch trees, forcing his way through the dusty, matted branches until he stumbled into a clearing, brushing needles from his hair.

Carys was sitting on a rock in the moonlight.

She had her back to him, and she made no sound, but he knew she had been crying bitterly; he could feel that, a raw urgency of grief and fury that made his palms sweat.

He stood, awkward.

After a while she raised her head. 'Well?'

'Felnia's all right.'

'I know that!' She turned, furious, her eyes red and sore.

He nodded. 'So is he. You could have killed him, but you didn't.'

'I wanted to!' She pushed her hair back; her face was taut and white. 'I really wanted to, Raffi. My mind was empty, except for hating him.'

'It's all right . . .'

'Don't be stupid!' Ripples of agitation slammed against him. 'Of course it's not all right! I wanted him dead. And Galen knows I did. I'm finished now, with the Watch and with you.' She laughed, bitterly. 'How did I get to this, Raffi? I thought I had everything under control.'

Quietly, he came forward. Standing opposite her he said, 'Come with us to Sarres.'

'Why? To be punished for my sins?'

'No. To be healed.'

Amazed, she stared at him. 'What?'

He chewed the ties of his jacket nervously. 'You've been hurt, Carys. You may not know it, but I can feel it. It's like a big emptiness in you. We can help . . . the Order has ways . . .'

'To forgive me?'

'That's not what I mean.'

She stood up quickly, brushing her hair back. 'You're soft, Raffi, that's your trouble. You'd never

208

survive without Galen. He won't want me along. He probably despises me.'

But something had changed in her. Raffi smiled. 'You don't know him.'

'I know he's hard as nails.'

'He's a Relicmaster. And it says in the Book that love is as fierce as hatred – as strong, and as reckless.'

She looked at him strangely. 'Does it? Perhaps that's why they never let us read all of it.'

She pushed past him through the larches. He trailed behind, catching the branches that swung back into his face.

At the campfire Galen was talking to the Sekoi, but when he saw them coming the keeper stood, tall and grim, his hawk-face half hidden in the shadows.

Carys walked right up to him and flung the crossbow down.

'You were right. It's not the way.'

His silence forced her to look up. 'All right, Galen,' she breathed. 'I missed him. I meant to. But . . .' Hopelessly, she shrugged. 'I'm sorry.'

'You don't feel sorry,' he said. 'You feel angry. And free.'

'I don't suppose you care what I feel.'

He laughed then, his rare, harsh laugh. 'The Order welcomes anyone, Carys. We have no failures either.'

She smiled. 'Even Watchspies?'

'Especially those.'

The Sekoi went to say something, but then waggled its long fingers and was silent.

Carys sat down. The fireglow made her look red and tired. 'I would have killed him once,' she said. 'Before I knew you, I probably wouldn't have thought twice. Now it's all more difficult.' She looked up, firmly. 'Look, I'll give you all the information you want. Everything. Numbers, passwords, details of patrols . . .'

'Carys.' The keeper crouched, his eyes dark in the flamelight. 'We don't want information. We want you. Will you come to Sarres?'

'Where is that?'

'Beyond your world. The place where the Order will begin again. The heart of the web, where we'll wait for the Makers. Will you come? We want you to come.'

She looked at him a long time, then away into the flames. 'I'll come. After all, where else can I go?'

Then, quickly, she reached into the pouch at her waist and brought out the relic, thrusting it into his hands. 'You'd better have this. I stole it from the Tower of Song. I think it's important.'

He stared at it in surprise, then at Raffi. 'Was this what you used for the net?'

'Yes.'

Galen clicked his tongue in annoyance. 'It'll have little power left, if any.' He spread his fingers over it. 'It feels faint.'

'So do I, sorceror.'

The voice was a snarl; Raffi jumped up, nervously.

Alberic had to be helped to the fire. Sikka brought a chair for him and placed it; the dwarf lowered himself into it as if he were an old man. His hair was thin, his face drawn with pain. His chest heaved, as if he had no breath. But he glared at Galen as furiously as ever.

'You've got what you want. Take the curse off.'

'And then?' Galen asked.

'Then I take my lads and lasses and clear out. Oh, and the Watchman. He's mine. You can have her.' He pointed a tiny finger at Carys. 'She won't fetch you much.'

'On the contrary.' Galen turned the relic over. 'She already has.'

The dwarf eyed it without interest. 'You people and your bits of junk. Well?'

Galen sat still, the moonlight falling on him. 'The curse has been on you a long time,' he said softly. 'How can I take it off?'

Alberic went rigid. 'By Flain, you'd better!' he hissed. 'Or you'll never leave this wood.'

Galen grinned. 'You mistake me.' He stood up suddenly, and leaned forward. 'You've read the Book, you told me once?'

'The Litany.' Alberic waved his fingers, painfully. 'Rather obscure style, I thought.'

'So you know about the Crow?'

'I've heard of it.'

'Now you can see it.'

Galen tossed the relic to Raffi; sparks were leaping from it. As he stood there, he seemed strangely taller; the darkness closed in about him. He reached over, caught Alberic's hand and pulled him upright. The dwarf stared, astonished, and as Galen looked down at him a sudden shiver of energy moved through their linked fingers, and in an instant of breathtaking clearness everyone saw it, the sharpness of the black eyes, the power that looked out of them, the abrupt shift that made the dark figure something else, something charged, out of myth, out of legend.

Alberic swore, snatching his hand away. Behind him his people stared.

Galen grinned.

'God, keeper,' the dwarf breathed. 'What are you?'

'I'm the Crow.' He said it quietly, and the ghost

211

images of seven moons drifted between his fingers.
'See it and believe it, thief-lord, because apart from
these, you're the first. Things are changing. The
Interrex is found, Anara will have a leader again.
And the Order has a home; we'll make it such a
powerhouse it will re-energize the world. Above
all, I've spoken with the Makers. The Makers are
coming back, Alberic.'

The dwarf swallowed. He stood up straight now,
breathed easy. 'Crackpot fanatics,' he muttered. 'I
almost believe it.'

'You should. Because I haven't finished with
you.'

'Oh no!' Alberic jumped back, instantly. 'Oh no.
I came looking for you once, but never again! I've
had my fill of sorcerors. From now on I'll avoid
you like fireseed, Galen Harn.'

Galen nodded darkly. 'That's what you think.'

He turned, took the relic from Raffi and held it
in both hands. It spat and crackled. Suddenly
it hummed, and the dwarf stepped closer, greedily.

Raffi stood up. To his amazement he saw the
tiny screen had lit, and words were racing across
it, minute white Maker-words that Galen hurriedly
began to read aloud.

'... Things are desperate; it may be we will
have to withdraw. There's been no word
from earth for months. Worst of all, we're
sure now about Kest. Against all orders, he's
tampered with the genetic material.
Somehow, he has made a hybrid out of what
was once a man ... Flain fears it has a
disturbed nature, certainly a greatly
enhanced lifespan ... When it was let out of
the chamber it destroyed all ...'

The screen flickered; Galen frowned and shook it
desperately.

'... We have flung it deep in the Pits of
        Maar. Kest called it the Margrave. We
        should have destroyed it. We should ...'
The screen went blank.

In the silence, only the fire crackled. Then Raffi
said, 'That was what I saw in the vision.'

'It's what rules the Watch,' Carys muttered in
disgust.

Slowly, Galen turned the relic over in his hands.
He seemed slightly dizzy. Finally he said, 'This may
tell us more. In Sarres, we might be able to restore
it in some way.' He looked at Raffi.

'It seems the Makers have spoken to us again.
How can they re-make the world if the most evil
of its creatures still lurks here?'

Worried, Raffi said, 'What can we do about
that?'

The keeper folded his arms. 'I don't know.'

It was dark in the wood now; the fire had sunk.
As the Sekoi piled wood on, the flames sparked
up and crackled. Alberic yelled at his people, 'Get
me something to eat! Plenty!'

He sat down by the Sekoi, who said idly, 'I
suppose there's no chance, now that you're cured,
of me getting my gold back?'

'Don't push your luck, tale-spinner. It's not half
what you stole from me.'

'And do you still want me as your prisoner?'

'Want you!' The dwarf put his face close up to
it, fiercely. 'I fully intend never to see any of you
scumbags again.'

Carys grinned, and Raffi smiled too. But then
he turned and saw Galen. The keeper had a dark,
thoughtful look.

Raffi knew it only too well.

It always meant trouble.

CATHERINE FISHER

THE RELIC MASTER

voLume 1 of the
book of the
C̃R⊗W̄

Raffi travels to the City of the Crow with his ailing
master Galen, the Relic Master. As the journey
progresses and Galen's powers diminish, Raffi has to
be wary of all strangers such as the enigmatic girl
Carys whom they meet as they draw closer to the
City of Destruction. Will the Relic Master be able
to summon the Crow to protect them in this
suspicious city? Or will the ever-present Watch
eliminate them along with so many others?

'The immemorial appeal of a quest story written by
an author firing on all cylinders.'

THE INDEPENDENT

ISBN   0099263939   £3.99

CATHERINE FISHER

FLAIN'S CORONET

VOLUME 3 OF THE
BOOK OF THE
CROW

Galen, Master of the Relics, is faced with a deadly
enemy, the Margrave, who is determined to stop the
return of the Makers. Galen knows that to defeat
this mighty, unknown force he must find the most
powerful of all the Makers' tools, the Coronet of
Flain. He and Raffi set out to find the lost Coronet
but their mission is dangerous and treachery follows
them like a shadow. Whom should they trust in
such unsettled times? Meanwhile, Carys struggles
to gain the trust of her companions as she tries to
put her past behind her.

'Catherine Fisher is an accomplished writer...'

BOOKS FOR KEEPS

ISBN   0099403064   £3.99

CATHERINE FISHER

THE MARGRAVE

volume 4 of the
BOOK OF THE
CROW

Every Nightmare Raffi's ever had is coming true.
He's too scared for the Deep Journey, Carys has
been captured, and worst of all, Galen has sworn a
terrible oath to destroy the deadly creature called
the Margrave, even if the quest takes them all into
the Pit of Maar itself. And far down there – below
the surface of the world, in the deepest darkness –
what evil thing is waiting for them to come?

'Catherine Fisher is a writer of rare talent'
THE SUNDAY TIMES

ISBN   0099404877   £3.99